PRAISE FOR AMANDA WILLS

'I enjoyed every second and barely put it down! Another great horsey read from one of my favourite pony authors.'

'I wish all teen books were more like Flick Henderson and the Deadly Game. It is a terrific read, with a twisty, engaging plot, just enough romance and lots of pets. I'm only sad I've finished reading it - bring back Flick!'

'Absolutely love this author.'

D1375389

THE THIRTEENTH HORSE

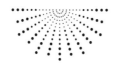

AMANDA WILLS

ISBN-13: 978-1977908834
ISBN-10: 1977908837

WANTED: ANIMAL LOVER

*K*risty Moore reached for her piggy bank and gave it a hopeful shake. Inside, coins jangled reassuringly. She had been saving for weeks. Would there be enough? She tugged open the plastic stopper and tipped the contents onto her bed, biting her bottom lip as she sorted the coins into piles and counted carefully. As she did she remembered all the odd jobs she'd carried out to earn the money. A pound a day for walking Mrs White's arthritic spaniel, Max, while she was laid up with the flu. Two pounds for washing Mr and Mrs James's filthy estate car. They'd seen Kristy coming a mile off. It cost five pounds in the car wash in town. Fifty paltry pence for weeding the whole of Mr Smith's front garden. She should have known better - Mrs White had warned her he was as mean as they come.

The piles of coins remained stubbornly small no matter how many times she re-arranged them. Kristy felt inside the piggy bank, just in case she'd missed a note or two, but no such luck. It was pathetic. She had worked for hours and hours and had earned the precise sum of seventeen pounds, twenty-three pence and a shiny silver button.

She sat slumped on the end of her bed and stared despondently at the piggy bank. A group lesson at Coldblow Equestrian Centre was twenty-five pounds. It would take her at least another three weeks to earn that. Three years, if miserly Mr Smith was paying her wages. It had been months since she'd last been near a horse, let alone had a chance to ride. And she was suffering as a consequence. She had a dull ache in her heart that wouldn't shift and a tendency to gaze glumly out of the nearest window when she should be concentrating in lessons. She was grumpy and impatient with her parents. They thought she missed their old house, their old life. But they were wrong. All she really missed were her riding lessons. She didn't need to visit a doctor to know what was wrong with her. She had serious horse withdrawal symptoms.

'Kristy, lunch is ready!' bellowed her mum, forgetting yet again that they lived in a tiny two-bedroomed apartment now, not a large, detached house with a massive garden and a view of the hills.

'Coming!' Kristy shoved the coins back into her piggy bank and left it on her bedside table, next to a photo of her riding Minty, her favourite pony at Coldblow.

Her dad was already sitting at the breakfast bar in the kitchen. They used to have a dining room in the old house, with fussy curtains, heavy oak furniture and an ornate chandelier. Kristy preferred eating at the breakfast bar. It was so much more cosy.

'Why the sad face?' he said.

Kristy slid into the seat next to him. 'You know all those odd jobs I've been doing for the neighbours?'

He nodded. 'You've worked really hard.'

'I *still* haven't got enough for a single riding lesson.'

He gave a sad smile. 'I'm sorry, sweetheart. I know this has been tough for you. Moving into the apartment, changing schools. If I could afford to pay for riding lessons, believe me I would.'

'I know you would. It's fine, honestly.' She smiled brightly. 'I just need to think of another way to earn money. I need a proper job.'

'What about a paper round?' suggested her mum, placing a plate in front of Kristy. 'They're advertising for paper boys and girls at the newsagent's around the corner.'

Kristy chewed thoughtfully. 'That could work. I could do it before school, couldn't I?'

'As long as your schoolwork doesn't suffer,' said her dad.

Kristy made up her mind. 'I'll go straight after lunch.'

∼

A MAN WITH A BROAD, deeply-lined forehead and a pen behind one ear was measuring out sweets for a boy aged about eight, who was jiggling coins in his pockets. Kristy waited for the boy to pay and gave the man a hopeful smile.

'I was wondering if you had any paper rounds going.'

'We certainly do. Have you ever done a paper round before?'

'No, but I'm a fast learner.'

'It's an early start. My paper boys and girls have to be here at six o'clock, seven days a week. Do you think you can manage that?'

'Sure. I'm an early bird,' said Kristy confidently.

'And do you have permission from your parents? I'd need them to sign a consent form.'

'Yes, they're cool with it.'

The man looked at her appraisingly. 'You seem very keen, I'll say that for you. Yes, I think I can offer you a week's trial and if it all goes well, the job is yours.'

Kristy felt like whooping with joy. Instead she smiled at the newsagent. 'Thanks. When do I start?'

He reached for a pile of forms on the counter behind him. 'Sorry, I forgot to check, you are thirteen, aren't you?'

Kristy felt a flicker of anxiety. It had been going so well. 'No. I'm twelve. Does it matter?'

The newsagent frowned. 'I'm afraid it does. Our paper boys and girls have to be thirteen. When's your birthday?'

'Not until the summer,' said Kristy gloomily.

'Then I can't offer you a job. Sorry, but I have to go by the rules.'

Kristy's shoulders drooped. 'It's OK. I understand. Thanks anyway.'

She trudged out of the shop.

'Come back in the summer!' the newsagent called after her. But it was no consolation. Kristy needed a job and she needed it now.

The door clicked shut behind her and she wrapped her scarf tightly around her neck. It was late autumn and a chill wind whipped mocha-brown leaves into eddies at her feet. She didn't feel like going home just yet. She thrust her hands into her pockets and stared despondently at the postcards in the shop window. Someone was advertising a secondhand bike, someone else had a litter of kittens for sale. Posters publicised coffee mornings, charity bike rides and musical concerts. Just as she turned to go a mud-stained card caught her eye:

Wanted: Animal-lover prepared to work long hours. Must be hard-working. Job satisfaction guaranteed! Call Emma Miller on...

It was a local number. Her curiosity aroused, Kristy ran into the shop and asked the newsagent if she could borrow his pen. He whipped it from behind his ear and she scribbled the number on the back of her hand.

'Is that Emma's number?' he asked.

Kristy nodded. 'I just saw the postcard.'

He laughed. 'She won't be too fussy about your age. As long as you can shift a bale of hay.'

As Kristy ambled back to the apartment she wondered who Emma Miller was and what kind of business she ran. Perhaps it was a cattery or a kennels. Or, if there was hay involved, maybe some sort of farm or petting zoo. Kristy didn't mind what animals she kept, as long as there weren't any snakes. Snakes freaked her out.

She ran lightly up the steps to their apartment and let herself in. Her parents looked up as she burst into the kitchen.

'Well, have you got a job?' asked her mum.

'Not yet. But I might do soon.'

Kristy took the phone into the hallway and punched in Emma Miller's number. The phone clicked and a woman's voice rang out.

'Hello!' boomed the voice.

'Hello,' said Kristy.

'Who is this?'

'Er, my name's Kristy. I saw your advert in the newsagent's. Are you still looking for a hard-working animal-lover?'

The woman roared with laughter. 'Why, are you volunteering?'

'I think so. I mean, definitely. Yes please. As long as it's not with snakes.'

'Snakes? What on earth makes you think I've got *snakes*?'

Kristy was glad Emma Miller couldn't see her pink cheeks. 'I was just checking.'

'I need someone who is strong and enthusiastic. Someone who's prepared to get their hands dirty. Someone who will follow instructions. Does that sound like you?'

Kristy wondered what she was letting herself in for. Then she remembered Minty and the other Coldblow ponies. 'It absolutely does.'

'Marvellous. Come over at three o'clock for a formal interview. And if you pass that, the job's yours.'

'Great, thanks. Wait! You haven't told me where to come.'

'Haven't I?' said Emma Miller distractedly. 'Silly me. We're at the top end of town, close to the park. Mill Farm Stables.'

Kristy felt a fizz tingle down her spine like she'd been hit by lightning. Did she say *stables*? She clutched the phone in a daze, and then stared into the handset as if it was a telescope and she'd be able to see a yard full of horses at the end of it if she looked hard enough. But the phone was revealing nothing and a little voice at the back of her head was telling her not to be so stupid. Of course Emma Miller hadn't said stables. She must have misheard.

She became aware of a tinny voice spilling out of the phone. There was only one way to find out. She held the handset close to her ear and said breathlessly, 'Did you say -'

'I'll see you at three,' said Emma Miller. And the line went dead.

2

MILL FARM STABLES

*K*risty skidded her bike to a halt and tried to calm her racing heart. She almost couldn't bring herself to read the blue sign at the end of the long gravel driveway. She squeezed her eyes shut, imagining for a few more blissful moments that she hadn't misheard Emma Miller, and that she was about to attend a job interview at an actual stables. But it was no good, she had to know one way or the other. She forced open one eye and scanned the swirly white lettering. *Mill Farm Stables. Four-star livery for horses and ponies. Proprietor Emma Miller.* Kristy re-read the sign with both eyes wide open, just to make sure. Mill Farm was still a stables and Kristy felt like the luckiest girl in the world.

She wheeled her bike along the drive to a cluster of wooden-slatted buildings at the other end. The yard was empty, save for a ginger cat who was curled up in a ball on a bale of shavings. Kristy checked her watch. She was ten minutes early. Her eyes tracked back and forth, taking in every detail. Stables flanked the yard on three sides and a long barn ran the length of the fourth. Behind the barn a much larger building loomed. Kristy guessed it was an indoor school. Buckets were piled up under an outside tap and empty haynets were coiled in a heap next to two bales of hay. Compared to Coldblow it was a little shabby around the edges. The concrete was crumbling in places and the emerald green stable doors needed a lick of paint. Coldblow had enormous loose boxes with automatic water drinkers, a horse walker, a solarium and a huge indoor arena. But Mill Farm felt unfussy and welcoming.

Kristy crossed the yard to the tap. She might as well make herself useful. She had filled all the buckets with water and had stuffed hay into six of the twelve haynets by the time a lean, blonde woman in a quilted jacket and jeans strode into the yard.

The woman stopped in her tracks. 'Kirsty?' she asked faintly, her eyebrows knotted in surprise.

'It's Kristy, actually,' said Kristy. 'I did get the right time, didn't I?'

'You certainly did.' The woman took in the filled water buckets and haynets. 'It's just that no-one has ever shown initiative before. I can't quite believe it. I'm Emma, by the way.'

'Pleased to meet you,' said Kristy politely, holding out her hand.

Emma pumped it enthusiastically and looked Kristy up and down. 'Have you looked after horses before?'

'Only imaginary ones in the garden when I was little,' Kristy admitted. 'But I'm used to handling horses. I used to have riding lessons, you see.'

Emma sighed. 'If it's free lessons you're after, you've come to the wrong place. This isn't a riding school. I look after other people's horses. I want a stablehand, not a working pupil.'

Kristy nodded vehemently. 'I know.'

'The last two girls I had were utterly useless. They had no

interest in mucking out. All they wanted to do was ride. The last one was so dizzy she forgot to tie up the gate and the horses escaped. Fortunately they hadn't reached the main road by the time I found them. I can't imagine what would have happened if they had.' Emma shuddered. 'The girl before that spent more time on her mobile than she did working. You don't have a phone, do you?'

Kristy had been pestering her parents for a phone for weeks. Suddenly she was glad they couldn't afford one. 'No.'

'Good.' Emma opened the door of the nearest stable. 'I'm going to set you a challenge. I want you to have a go at mucking out. If I think you show potential, the job's yours.'

Kristy peered into the gloomy stable. It was a mess. She'd never mucked out before. Not that she minded getting her hands dirty. She loved nothing more than spending a morning with her granddad, digging on his allotment. But the more she stared at the dirty bed of straw the more she realised she didn't have a clue where to start.

Emma must have seen the panic on her face.

'Don't worry, I won't stand here and watch. I'll be back in half an hour. That should give you plenty of time.'

She disappeared into the barn leaving Kristy still staring at the stable, hoping for inspiration. She pictured her pet rabbit Bugs in his hutch on their narrow balcony. She mucked him out religiously every day. Surely the principal was the same when you mucked out a stable, just on a much larger scale?

She went in search of a wheelbarrow and pitchfork and began forking out the muck and wet straw. Minty's stable at Coldblow had thick banks of straw around the sides to stop her lying too close to the walls and getting cast. Kristy banked the clean, dry straw around the edges and while the floor dried she emptied the wheelbarrow onto the enormous muck heap at the back of the barn.

'The straw's in here,' called Emma as Kristy pushed the wheelbarrow past the barn's huge double doors. Kristy filled the wheelbarrow and wheeled it back to the stable. Using the fork, she shook the straw out, making a deep bed that looked so inviting she could have happily curled up and slept in it herself.

She was carrying over a water bucket and haynet when Emma reappeared. She stood in the doorway, her hands on her hips, inspecting Kristy's handiwork. After what seemed like hours Emma turned to her with a smile. 'If that's the first time you've mucked out a stable, then I am very impressed. I am happy to say the job of lowly stablehand is yours. If you still want it?'

'I'd love it!' cried Kristy.

'The hours are four to six on weeknights and nine to three on Saturdays. You can have Sundays off. And, believe me, you'll need it.'

Kristy knew she was grinning like an idiot but she couldn't help herself. It had something to do with the smell of horse that filled her nostrils and the sound of the occasional whinny from the paddocks. The dull ache in her heart had melted away like ice-cream on a hot summer's day and she felt content for the first time in months.

Emma closed the stable door. 'I'll give you a quick tour of the yard, introduce you to all the horses and show you your duties.'

The tack room was a large, square room with a vaulted roof, two small windows and wood-panelled walls. Two of the walls were lined with saddle racks. Bridles and headcollars hung from hooks on a third. A moth-eaten three-seater sofa and two equally tatty armchairs were arranged around a wooden crate that doubled up as a coffee table. A kettle and a motley collection of mugs sat on a wide shelf and in the far corner was an old black stove, in which a log crackled and spat.

'This is cosy,' said Kristy, thinking of the immaculate but functional tack room at Coldblow.

'It's seen better days. But it's warm and dry. The kids like to hang out here after they've ridden. You can join them, as long as you've finished all your jobs.'

Emma took a headcollar and lead rope from a hook. 'We look after twelve horses and ponies here at Mill Farm. You'll be responsible for the three ponies, Silver, Copper and Jazz. You just mucked out Silver's stable. Copper and Jazz's stables are either side of his. Which school do you go to?'

Puzzled by the change of subject, Kristy said, 'The high school. Why?'

'You might know their owners, Norah, William and Sofia.'

'I haven't been there long. We've only just moved to this side of town.' Kristy didn't add that she still hadn't made any friends at her new school. Emma didn't need to know that.

'Well, you'll meet them next week. That's Silver.' She pointed to a rotund dappled grey pony. He bustled over to them and began nibbling Emma's pockets. She laughed. 'All he thinks about is his stomach. There's Jazz.' A pretty palomino mare with four white socks looked up at the sound of her name.

'She's beautiful,' said Kristy.

'And very highly strung,' said Emma. 'Copper is the chestnut gelding grazing by the water trough. He's a darling. As steady as they come.'

They toured the paddocks, meeting all the horses. Kristy tried to memorise their names and listened carefully as Emma ran through her list of jobs. She was to muck out all three ponies' stables, give them fresh hay and water, bring them in from the field and change their rugs. If they weren't being ridden she was also to give them a quick groom and pick out their feet.

'Have you ever done that before?' Emma asked.

Kristy shook her head. 'Sorry.'

'Don't be.' Emma handed her the headcollar. 'You catch Silver and I'll show you what to do.'

Kristy called softly to the grey gelding and approached him quietly.

'Loop the lead rope over his neck to stop him wandering off,' said Emma. Kristy did as she was told and was relieved when Silver stood patiently while she slid the noseband over his muzzle and buckled the headpiece. She clicked her tongue and the gelding followed her out of the field. Emma showed her how to tie a quick release knot, pick out his feet and change his rug.

'You'll soon get the hang of it.'

'Shall I turn him back out?' said Kristy.

'Yes please. But put him in the bottom paddock, would you? There's less grass in there. He's fat enough as it is.'

Kristy led Silver past the other horses and ponies to the bottom paddock. At first, she thought it was empty. But as she undid Silver's headcollar she saw a movement in the corner of her eye. She gave a little start. A black horse was watching her from the far corner of the paddock. He was as sturdy as a Shire horse, but not as tall, with a narrow blaze shaped like a bolt of lightning and a thick forelock that was so long it covered one eye like a curtain.

'But I've met all twelve horses,' Kristy said to Silver. He gave her a friendly nudge and wandered off to graze. Kristy watched the black horse for a while longer, wondering who he belonged to and why Emma hadn't mentioned him.

When her fingers were numb with cold she retraced her steps back to the yard. Emma was nowhere to be seen. Kristy waited for a while, wondering what to do. And then she saw a note pinned to the tack room door. *Had to go and get horse feed. See you Monday. Four o'clock sharp!*

Kristy pulled on her gloves, retrieved her bike and took one last look at Mill Farm Stables. Working here would be hard work, there was no doubt about that. And Emma hadn't even mentioned how much a lowly stablehand was paid. But Kristy realised she didn't care. The truth was, she would happily work for free if it meant she could get a regular horse fix.

It wasn't until that night, when she was lying in bed going over the events of the day, that she remembered the mysterious thirteenth horse. He'd looked lost, standing there all alone, an outsider looking in. She knew how he felt, and her heart twisted painfully.

3
MYSTERY HORSE

Kristy fought her way through the jostling groups of children leaving the canteen and headed towards the library. The rest of her year were streaming out onto the playing fields, where they would pass the rest of their lunch hour playing ball or laughing and joking with their friends.

Normally Kristy would tag behind them and watch from a safe distance, hoping that one day someone might notice her and ask her to join in. It hadn't happened yet, but she lived in hope. But from now on she would be spending every lunchtime in the library. She had no choice. When she'd told her parents the hours she would be working at Mill Farm they'd hit the roof.

'You've said you'll work every day after school? What about your homework?' her mum had cried.

'You didn't mind me getting a paper round,' Kristy reasoned.

'That would have been an hour before school, not two hours afterwards. *And* all day Saturday,' said her dad.

'I'll spend lunchtimes in the library doing homework and catch up with the rest on Sundays,' she said.

Her parents looked at each other but said nothing.

She had a brainwave. 'Parents' evening is in four weeks' time. If my grades have dropped I promise I'll give up the job. But if they haven't, you have to promise me that I can carry on working.'

Her dad took off his glasses and rubbed the bridge of his nose. Kristy held her breath.

'Alright. We'll give it four weeks. But if your schoolwork suffers you'll have to stop. Understood?'

'Understood,' said Kristy, and she'd darted out of the room before they could change their minds.

Kristy found a table near a window and laid out her pencil case and exercise books. She was halfway through a long and complicated maths worksheet when a tall girl with dark red shoulder-length hair approached the table.

'Mind if I sit here?' she asked.

Kristy smiled. 'Not at all.'

The red-haired girl pulled up a chair opposite Kristy and fished a battered paperback out of her bag. A pewter-coloured horse galloped across the cover, its mane and tail flowing like molten silver. The girl was soon completely engrossed in her book.

Kristy, meanwhile, was finding it hard to concentrate on the factors and equations she was supposed to be solving. She stole glances at the red-haired girl. She looked older than Kristy and was probably in the year above her. Kristy wondered why she was spending her lunch hour on her own, too.

Kristy pushed the worksheet away and sighed. She'd had loads of friends at her old school and couldn't work out why she wasn't making friends here. But joining halfway through the first term meant that everyone already had their friendship groups sorted and, no matter how hard she tried, there didn't seem to be any room for Kristy to join them.

The bell for lessons sounded and Kristy shoved her pencil case and half-finished worksheet into her rucksack. She checked her timetable. History in the humanities block and then PE. When she looked up again the red-haired girl was disappearing through the door. But in her haste to leave she'd left her book on the table.

Kristy grabbed it and ran after her. She caught up with her in the corridor that led to the canteen.

'Hey,' Kristy said, tapping the girl on the shoulder. She spun around in surprise.

'You left your book in the library.'

The girl hit her forehead with the heel of her hand and laughed. 'I'm hopeless. I'd forget my head if it wasn't screwed on. Thank you so much.'

'No problem,' said Kristy.

'See you around,' said the red-haired girl, plunging into the torrent of schoolchildren on their way to lessons. Kristy hitched her rucksack further up her shoulder, cast one last look back at the girl, and made her way towards the humanities block.

KRISTY GLANCED at her watch as she jogged along the driveway to Mill Farm Stables. It was two minutes to four. She'd whipped like a tornado through the apartment when she'd arrived home from school, flinging down her rucksack, throwing on her jeans and a fleece jacket and grabbing a banana from the fruit bowl to keep her going until supper time. It had been a crazy rush, but she'd managed it.

Emma was giving a girl a leg up onto the pretty palomino mare with the four white socks. Jazz, Kristy thought to herself. Beautiful and highly-strung. The girl tightened her girth and turned the mare towards the indoor school. As she passed Kristy she did a double take.

'The girl in the library!' she screeched so loudly that her pony skittered sideways and almost knocked Emma flying.

'Careful!' Emma cried, grabbing hold of the reins and steadying Jazz.

But the girl wasn't listening. 'You saved my life today. I would have literally cried myself to sleep tonight if I'd lost that book. It's my favourite in the whole world. I've read it like a thousand times. What are you doing here, Library Girl?'

'Kristy's my new stablehand,' said Emma.

'I'm Sofia,' said the girl. 'And this is my pony Jazz. I'm afraid she's as ditzy as I am.'

Kristy stroked the mare's neck. 'She's absolutely gorgeous.'

'I hate to interrupt, but you have half an hour in the school before I need to use it, Sofia. And you still have three stables to muck out, Kristy.'

Sofia rolled her eyes. 'You're so bossy, Emma. You'd have made a great teacher.' She winked at Kristy, who couldn't help smiling back.

'The thought of a classroom full of children is enough to send me running for the hills. Dealing with you and the twins is bad enough,' Emma replied tartly. 'Now go and exercise your pony before I really lose my patience.'

Sofia chuckled and kicked Jazz into a trot.

'And how many times have I told you not to trot in the yard!' Emma yelled after her.

Kristy set to work, mucking out Jazz's stable first so it would be ready for the mare once Sofia had finished riding. By the time she had finished mucking out all three stables she had shed her fleece and could feel a sheen of perspiration on her brow. She was filling the ponies' haynets when Sofia led Jazz into the yard.

Sofia peered over Jazz's stable door. 'That looks great, Kristy. Thank you.'

'No problem.'

Sofia ran up her stirrup leathers and loosened Jazz's girth. 'You're new at school, right?'

'Yes, we only moved here in September. I'm in the year below you, I think.'

'Then you're in the same year as the Bergman twins. Norah and William. Copper and Silver are their ponies. Do you know them?'

'I don't think so.'

'You'd know if you did. Norah is even bossier than Emma, and William is so laid back he's virtually horizontal. They don't ride on Mondays but you'll meet them tomorrow.'

Kristy tied up Jazz's haynet and filled her water bucket while Sofia untacked her. 'I'll fetch her rug,' Kristy said.

'No, I'll do that. You've got enough to do.'

'Thanks. It's all taking me a bit longer than I thought it would,' she admitted.

'You'll soon speed up. I'd love to do more to look after Jazz but my dad would go mad if he found out he was paying for me to muck out my own pony.' Sofia flicked a body brush over her mare's glossy coat and rugged her up. 'Do you ride?'

'I used to have lessons but I had to stop when we moved.'

'That's a shame. Where did you ride?'

'Coldblow. It's on the other side of town.'

Sofia gave a sharp intake of breath. 'Goodness, you didn't tell Emma that, did you?'

'No. She never asked. Why?'

'Coldblow is owned by her sister Karen. They fell out

years ago. Karen is always poaching owners from Emma. They can't stand the sight of each other.'

'But Coldblow is nothing like Mill Farm. It's -' Kristy broke off, embarrassed.

'Smart and posh?' Sofia grinned.

'Well, yes,' said Kristy. 'Although I much prefer it here,' she added hurriedly.

'You're right, Coldblow is much swankier. But Karen's in it for the money. She doesn't care about the horses like Emma does. I wouldn't want to keep Jazz anywhere else.'

Once Jazz, Copper and Silver were settled in their stables, Kristy walked down to the bottom paddock. She wanted to see if the black horse was still there. She counted the others as she went. There were definitely twelve. Why hadn't Emma mentioned him? He was standing under a tree, dozing, but looked up when he heard the gate click open.

He turned to watch her as she picked a handful of grass and walked towards him. He was big, about 15hh, with a proud, arched neck and a wide chest. He whickered a welcome and Kristy's heart melted.

'Here you are,' she said softly, holding out her palm. His whiskers tickled her hand as he nibbled the grass. 'Who do you belong to?' she murmured, stroking his broad face. He blew into her neck. She giggled, tracing his narrow blaze with her index finger. 'I've got to go now, but I'll be back, I promise.'

Kristy tramped back across the field. When she reached the gate, she looked back at the gelding. He was watching her intently, his head tilted at an almost comical angle.

She blew him a kiss. 'Goodbye, mystery horse. I'll see you tomorrow.'

4

FRIENDS AND ENEMIES

Kristy couldn't get the black gelding out of her head. He dominated her thoughts as she fidgeted her way through double maths and she doodled pictures of him in the margins of her exercise book when she should have been drawing a glacier in geography. She wanted to know everything about him. Who he belonged to, why Emma hadn't mentioned him. Was he even real? She'd woken up wondering if she'd imagined him. Perhaps, she thought with horror, he was a dream horse, as insubstantial as an almost-forgotten memory.

She sat in the library after lunch with her English text-book open in front of her, but spent more time watching the door for Sofia than she did memorising the list of spellings she was supposed to be learning for a test the next day. Just when she'd given up hope that the older girl was coming, Sofia scurried in, saw Kristy and slipped into the seat beside her.

'I would have been here earlier but I lost my trainers and we've got PE next,' she said, flicking her long fringe out of her eyes. 'How did you enjoy your first day at Mill Farm?'

Kristy showed Sofia her nails, which were engrained with dirt. 'I spent twenty minutes scrubbing them this morning, *and* I've got blisters on both hands. But I'm not complaining. I loved it.'

'Emma can be a bit strict, but her bark is worse than her bite, and she seems to have taken a shine to you,' said Sofia.

Kristy flushed with pleasure. 'I like her too. Sofia, you know that black gelding at Mill Farm?'

'Henry the Friesian?' Sofia asked. 'Isn't he beautiful?'

'No, not Henry.' Emma had introduced Kristy to Henry's owner the previous evening. 'The big horse down in the bottom paddock. With the long forelock and the lightning-shaped blaze.'

Sofia shook her head. 'Sorry, I don't ever go down there. Jazz is always in one of the top paddocks. Why?'

Before Kristy could answer the bell sounded. Sofia jumped to her feet and looked around her wildly. 'I mustn't forget my trainers!' she said, grabbing a carrier bag from under the table.

'See you at the stables tonight?' Kristy asked.

'Of course,' she grinned, dashing out of the library.

It wasn't until she'd gone that Kristy realised Sofia had left her schoolbag on the seat bedside her. She gave a resigned smile, picked up the bag and went in search of her new friend.

Kristy raced over to the stables after school and found Emma in the tack room, cleaning a saddle. 'Who is the black horse in the bottom paddock?' she asked breathlessly, before Emma had a chance to say hello.

'You mean Cassius?'

It was a noble name, Kristy thought. It suited him. 'Why

didn't you mention him when you were showing me all the horses?'

Emma scratched her head. 'Probably because he lives out all year.'

'Who does he belong to?'

Emma shrugged. 'No-one.'

'He must belong to someone!'

'Well, legally he belongs to me. But I didn't buy him. I just acquired him.'

'What do you mean?'

Emma dipped her sponge into the tin of saddle soap and rubbed it over the cantle. 'His owner did a moonlight flit.'

'A what?'

'She owed me six months in fees and the vet a small fortune. Then she disappeared one day without paying either of us a penny. Legally Cassius is mine in lieu of the money she owed me. I tried selling him, without much luck.'

'Why not?' said Kristy. 'He's so handsome.'

'Yes, but who wants a blind horse?'

Kristy felt the ground shift beneath her feet. '*Blind?*'

'Well, blind in one eye. He had an eye infection and lost the sight in his right eye. Didn't you notice?'

Kristy remembered the way Cassius had tilted his head to watch her. She'd thought it was an endearing habit. 'The poor thing!'

'He's alright. Horses adapt very well to losing their sight. And he still has one good eye.'

'Did she used to ride him, his old owner?' Kristy asked.

'Why all the questions?'

'I just wondered.'

'Yes, she did. Not all cold-bloods are suitable for riding, but Cassius is a Percheron and they make lovely riding horses.'

'You mean he's cold-blooded, like a lizard? Or a snake?' Kristy shivered.

Emma laughed. 'No! Horses are mammals, they are all warm-blooded, but they fall into three categories: hot-bloods, cold-bloods and warmbloods. Hot-bloods were originally bred for racing and long-distance riding. Think of fiery Arabs or Thoroughbreds. Cold-bloods are classed as working horses and were bred for their strength and calm temperament, like Shires or Clydesdales.'

'And warmbloods are produced by crossing hot and cold-blooded horses?' Kristy guessed.

'That's right. Hanoverians, Holsteiners and Trakheners are all warmbloods.' Emma lifted the saddle back onto its rack. 'Cassius is a registered Percheron, although he's small for his breed. They can make 17hh.'

'Gentle giants,' said Kristy, remembering how he had taken the grass so delicately from her outstretched palm.

'They are,' Emma agreed. 'And I will try re-advertising him in the New Year. But who's going to buy a one-eyed horse when there are so many two-eyed ones for sale?'

Kristy pictured the big black gelding standing like a statue in the bottom paddock. *I would*, she thought wistfully.

KRISTY WAS PUSHING a wheelbarrow laden with hay across the yard when a bloodcurdling scream ripped through the air. She jumped and the wheelbarrow wobbled and tipped over, scattering hay all over the newly-swept yard.

'William!' shrieked a voice. It appeared to be coming from Silver's stable.

Someone behind Kristy hooted with laughter. She turned to see a tall, skinny boy with a bridle over one shoulder and his long, thin arms looped under a saddle.

'I swapped Silver's girth for a shorter one so she'd think he'd got even fatter,' he stage-whispered to Kristy, his eyes glinting with mischief.

'I heard that!' screeched the voice. A small, sturdy girl with a curly blonde bob stomped out of the stable straight past Kristy. She drew herself up to her full height, which was still only just about level with the boy's shoulders, and poked him in the chest. 'I have had enough of your stupid pranks, William Bergman!'

William grinned at Kristy. 'I thought it was inspired but sadly my sister was born without a sense of humour. You must be Kristy. Sofia said you were the new stablehand.'

'Where've you hidden my girth?' yelled Norah, completely ignoring Kristy.

William pointed a thumb in the direction of the tack room. 'It's in the box with the travel boots.'

Norah spun on her heels and stomped off. A few seconds later she re-appeared with a navy girth clutched in her hands. She glared at her brother. 'Wait 'til I tell Mum.'

'I'm trembling in my boots,' said William. 'Now, are you going to get over your strop and come and ride with me or not?'

'I don't have any choice, do I, seeing as we've only got the indoor school until five,' she said. She looked at Kristy, who was darting about trying to catch wisps of hay before they were blown all over the yard. 'You are going to wet that before you give it to Silver, aren't you? He has a dust allergy. I'm sure Emma must have told you.'

Taken aback by the girl's imperious tone, Kristy found herself bobbing her head deferentially. 'Yes, I'm just about to do it,' she muttered, grabbing the last piece of hay by Norah's leather-booted feet. 'Sorry,' she gabbled. 'I'll get out of your way now.'

She had wheeled the barrow over to the tap when Norah's piercing voice rang out again.

'Hey, wait a minute, I know you, don't I?'

Kristy's hand froze centimetres from the tap.

'You're the new girl at school, aren't you?' Norah nodded to herself. 'Yes, I thought I recognised you. What are you doing working here?'

Kristy feigned a smile. 'I needed a job, Emma needed a stablehand. So here I am.'

Norah looked her up and down and then pointed at the hay. 'Well, make sure that gets a proper soak. I'll know whose fault it is if Silver starts coughing again.' And with that she turned on her heels and flounced back to the stable.

KRISTY FILLED the last of the water buckets and carried them carefully across the yard, trying not to splash water onto her boots. She looked at her watch and smiled with satisfaction. It was a quarter past six. She'd been a whole fifteen minutes faster than she had the previous day. She remembered the carrots she'd brought for the black gelding. Cassius, she corrected herself. She'd left them in a bag in the tack room. If she was quick she could run down to the paddock to see him and still be home in time for supper.

The door to the tack room was closed. Behind it Kristy could hear chatter and laughter. She hesitated outside, not wanting to intrude. And then she heard the familiar sound of Sofia's voice and she pushed the door open.

'Kristy!' Sofia cried, 'I was just coming to find you. Do you want a drink?'

Kristy rocked back on her heels. William was sprawled on one of the armchairs, peering at his mobile phone. 'Sofia makes an awesome hot chocolate,' he said, his eyes not leaving the screen.

His sister sat on one end of the sofa, her back rigid, and said nothing. Kristy could sense Norah didn't want her muscling in.

'Maybe another time? I promised Mum I'd be home by half-past.' She grabbed her bag, shouted a goodbye and raced down to the bottom paddock, suddenly desperate to see Cassius.

He was standing by the gate, as if he'd known she was coming. He cocked his head so he could watch her with his good eye. She rubbed his blaze and drank in every detail of him. The tufts of hair poking out of his smoky black ears; the snip of pink on his muzzle; his strong, broad chest; his right eye, which was slightly cloudy, like a wind-whipped sea. She threw her arms around him and buried her face in his neck. He smelled delicious, of meadow grass and warm horse. Her aching back, her blisters, Norah's hostility, all faded as she clung to him. He made her feel safe and content, yet she felt absurdly protective of him. One thing she knew for sure - she never wanted to let him go.

5

WAR HORSE

'*D*id you hear me, Kristy Moore?'

Mr Baker's voice cut through Kristy's daydream like an arrow and she shot up in her seat and looked at him guiltily.

'No, I'm sorry, Mr Baker. I didn't.'

'One lunchtime detention for you, young lady.' Their teacher narrowed his eyes and surveyed the class. 'I'll repeat myself for all those who were not paying attention the first time. For homework, I want you all to choose a subject you don't know much about, research it and write me a five-hundred word essay on it. By tomorrow. Class dismissed.'

The groans from the class were barely drowned out by the noise of scraping chairs as they filed out of the class-room. Mr Baker's reputation as the strictest teacher in the school was well-deserved, and it wasn't the first time Kristy had felt the sharp end of his tongue.

The essay was forgotten by the time she arrived at Mill Farm. She found Emma mixing feeds in the barn.

'Sofia and the twins don't usually ride on a Wednesday so you've got a nice peaceful shift,' said Emma.

Kristy felt a surge of relief that she wouldn't have to see Norah.

'If I get my jobs done in time, would I be able to give Cassius a groom?'

Emma tipped a scoop of pony nuts into a bucket and stretched her back. 'I don't see why not. He's very easy to handle. Remember to approach him from his good eye so he can see you. And be careful he doesn't accidentally stand on your foot. He weighs a ton.'

Kristy raced through her jobs, mucking out the ponies in record time. She had brought them in, changed their rugs and given them their feeds by a quarter to six. She ran into the tack room and found Cassius's headcollar hanging from a peg behind the door. It was enormous. She grabbed the carrot she'd brought from home and sprinted down to the bottom paddock.

The big black gelding was grazing in the far corner of the field. Kristy called him and his head shot up. When he saw who it was he whinnied. Kristy vaulted over the gate and crossed the field in a few strides. Cassius crunched the carrot noisily and held his head low so she could slip the headcollar over his nose, but she still had to stand on tiptoes to fasten the headpiece.

'I'll walk on your left side so you can see me,' she told him. In the yard she gave him a haynet and set to work, brushing the mud from his thick winter coat. When she realised there was no way she could reach his rump, she lugged over the mounting block and stood on that. She kept up a steady stream of chatter, telling him what she was going to do next. She was especially careful on his blind side so he knew where she was and what she was doing.

She combed his mane and brushed the knots and burrs from his tail. He didn't have thick feathers like other heavy horses she'd seen. His hooves, however, were huge. As big as dinner plates. Kristy wasn't sure she would even be able to lift them, let alone pick out his feet, but when she ran her hand down his near foreleg he picked up his foot immediately and shifted his weight so he wasn't leaning on her. She laughed with pleasure. 'You are a perfect gentleman, Cassius.'

'Shouldn't you be gone?' said Emma, appearing beside her. 'It's gone half past six.'

Kristy's hand flew to her mouth. Her mum would be furious if she wasn't home in time for supper.

Emma patted the gelding's neck. 'I'll turn him back out. You'd better scram. I don't want my favourite stablehand getting into trouble.'

'I'm your only stablehand,' said Kristy.

'Exactly!' said Emma, waggling a finger at her. 'I'll see you tomorrow.'

Kristy kissed Cassius's soft-as-velvet nose, waved goodbye to Emma and ran all the way home. Her mum was dishing up as she flew through the door, gabbling apologies. She didn't remember the essay until after they'd finished eating. Her heart sank. Mr Baker would go mad if she was late handing it in.

She gave her parents what she hoped was an ingratiating smile. 'I'll clear up tonight.'

'Thank you. That would be lovely,' said her mum.

'Afterwards, can I use the laptop?'

'You know the rules, Kristy. No screens after seven o'clock.'

'But it's for homework. It's got to be in first thing.'

Her mum sighed. 'Alright. Just for half an hour. But if this job keeps interfering with your schoolwork we are going to have to have a rethink, OK?'

'You promised you'd give it four weeks!' Kristy cried. 'You can't go back on your word. That's not fair!'

'Watch your attitude, Kristy Moore,' said her dad from behind his newspaper.

'Sorry, Mum,' Kristy muttered. 'Can I take it into my room? I can't concentrate with the television on.'

Her mum, who missed their big detached home with its book-lined study, sighed loudly. 'Of course.'

Kristy sat down at her desk and gazed blankly at the laptop. Research a subject she didn't know much about, Mr Baker had said. But what? She looked around for inspiration. She might as well choose a subject she was interested in. Her eyes rested on the photo of Minty on her bedside table. She felt so involved in life at Mill Farm Stables that her days at Coldblow seemed like an eternity ago. An image of Cassius popped into her head. She grinned. Of course, it was obvious! Googling Percheron, she reached in her rucksack for her exercise book, unscrewed the lid of her fountain pen and started to read.

Soon she was mesmerised. She'd had no idea Percherons originated from France and were first bred as war horses. The thought of Cassius galloping into battle, his mane and tail flying, made her insides go cold. Later, they were used to pull stagecoaches. Later still, they worked on farms pulling ploughs. Kristy wasn't surprised to discover that they were known in the heavy horse world for their intelligence and their placid nature. They were powerful yet gentle, and they made awesome riding horses. Kristy sucked the end of her pen and wondered what Cassius would be like to ride. Like a giant rocking horse, she decided. Smooth and steady with a comfortable, rhythmic canter and a long, loping walk. She filled line after line of her exercise book and it took her no time at all to reach five hundred words. She closed the laptop down with a satisfied sigh. Who knew homework could actually be fun?

6

SECRET RIDER

*K*risty woke early on Saturday morning, itching to be at Mill Farm. She bolted down her breakfast and pedalled furiously over to the stables, arriving an hour early.

Emma had warned her that Saturdays were the busiest day at the yard as owners took advantage of the weekend to ride in the indoor school or hack out and Kristy wanted to groom Cassius before she started work.

The night before Emma had given Kristy a list of her Saturday duties. After she had mucked out the ponies, she was to clean their tack. Her final job was to poo pick the four top paddocks and scrub and refill the water troughs.

'I need to stock up on shavings so you'll be on your own until about half nine. I'll feed them and turn them out before I go,' Emma had said.

It was a cold, bright day and Kristy could see her breath in clouds as she marched down to the bottom paddock. Cassius was waiting for her by the gate and she slipped on his headcollar. No-one was about. She realised in her haste she was still wearing her cycling helmet. She was about to unstrap it when she had an idea. She shook her head. It was out of the question. She scratched the gelding's poll and dithered. Could she? No-one would ever know. Cassius gave her gentle nudge, as if he knew exactly what she was thinking, and she led him beside the gate before she could change her mind. He stood serenely as she scrambled onto the top rung of the gate. He still looked impossibly tall, but if she grabbed a handful of his mane she reckoned she would make it. She cast one final look over her shoulder. There was still no-one about. And, before she knew it, she had jumped onto his back.

Kristy had ridden bareback a couple of times at Coldblow, and had always felt as if she could easily slip and fall off, no matter how hard she gripped with her knees. But that had been on small, narrow riding school ponies like Minty. She might as well be comparing jet skis to a cruise ship. Cassius was so broad and solid it was like sitting atop the most comfortable armchair in the world. She felt totally balanced and utterly safe.

Holding the end of the lead rope in one hand and a hank of mane in the other, Kristy squeezed with her legs. 'Good boy,' she murmured as he set off at a rolling walk around the paddock. His ears were pricked and his neck was arched. Kristy knew he was enjoying himself as much as she was. He probably hadn't been ridden for months, maybe even years, yet he responded to her leg aids when she asked him to change direction, and stood squarely when she reluctantly decided she had better get off.

Kristy led him up to the yard and tied him up outside the barn. She ducked into the tack room to find his grooming kit and almost jumped out of her skin when a figure sprang from nowhere.

'Nice ride?' said an acidic voice. Kristy's heart sank. It was Norah.

'I don't know what you're talking about,' she blustered.

'Does Emma know you've been sneaking rides on her horse?' Norah continued smoothly.

Kristy felt a flush creep up her neck.

'No, I didn't think so. I think someone should tell her, don't you? Although I don't think she's going to be very impressed.'

Kristy flinched as if she'd been hit. She loved working at Mill Farm and was slightly in awe of the indomitable Emma Miller. The thought of her new boss's disappointed face when she realised Kristy was just the latest in her long line of useless stablehands was too awful to contemplate.

'Please don't say anything. It was only once and I won't do it again,' Kristy said.

'I'm sorry, but I think I have a duty to,' Norah said regretfully.

Kristy noticed a small, self-righteous smile playing on Norah's lips and anger stirred inside her. She had always hated bullies.

'Actually, it's fine,' she said loudly. 'I'll tell Emma as soon as she's back. Save you the trouble,' she added, smiling sweetly.

A flicker of surprise wiped the smirk from Norah's face and she opened her mouth to protest. But Kristy had grabbed Cassius's grooming kit and fled into the yard before she could utter a word.

TELLING EMMA she had ridden Cassius behind her back was the hardest thing Kristy had ever had to do. Her limbs felt as heavy as lead as she dragged herself around the yard, looking for her boss. She found her raking the surface in the indoor school.

'Has someone died?' Emma asked, seeing the woebegone look on her face.

'No, but you might wish someone had when I tell you what I've done.' She took a deep breath. 'I rode Cassius in the field today.'

'You did *what?*' Emma spluttered.

'I couldn't help myself. The idea just popped into my head when I went to groom him, and it wouldn't go away. It was like an itch that had to be scratched,' Kristy said earnestly.

'An itch?' Emma repeated faintly.

'But it's no excuse, I know. I should have ignored the itch. He's not mine to ride.'

'I don't understand. You took his tack down to the field?'

Kristy shook her head. 'Just his headcollar. It was a spur of the moment thing. I rode him bareback around the field a few times.'

'No riding hat?'

'I had my cycling helmet on. I'm so, so sorry, Emma, and I promise it won't ever happen again.'

'Too right it won't.' Emma exhaled loudly. 'What if you'd fallen off and hurt yourself? What would I have told your parents? I'm responsible for you while you're here, Kristy. That's why I have rules. I don't make them up for the sheer hell of it.'

Kristy hung her head in shame. 'I know, and I totally understand if you want to let me go.'

Convinced she was about to get the sack, Kristy didn't take in Emma's next words at first.

'I said,' said Emma patiently, 'if you wanted to ride him so badly you should have just asked.'

'But -'

'Goodness knows he needs the exercise. I'm never going to sell him straight from the field. But if you get him fit I might stand a chance.'

Kristy gaped at Emma. 'Do you mean -?'

'Yes, you can ride Cassius. But there are conditions. You must finish your work first. You must take things slowly - he's very unfit. And you must only ever ride him when I'm here. OK?'

Kristy flung her arms around her boss. 'I don't know what to say! Thank you so much. You don't know what this means to me.'

Emma patted Kristy gingerly on the shoulder. 'I may be getting on a bit but I do remember what it's like to be twelve and horse-mad. Now, do you have your own riding hat?'

Kristy swallowed the large lump that had mysteriously appeared in her throat. 'I do, thank you.'

'Why don't you whizz home in your lunch hour and get it. Then you can have a ride this afternoon if you like. The school's free at four for half an hour.'

'Are you sure?' said Kristy, her eyes shining. She deserved a dressing down yet Emma had not only given her a second chance, she had offered Kristy the one thing she craved. She couldn't believe her good luck.

'Yes. Now go and finish mucking out before I change my mind!'

~

EMMA FOUND Cassius's saddle and bridle and helped her tack up.

'Remember to always approach him on his good side so he can see you, and talk to him so he knows you're there. He'll be fine on the right rein but he might be a bit spooky on the left rein. Let him turn his head to see where strange sights or sounds are coming from,' Emma said, giving Kristy a leg-up. She patted the gelding's neck. 'Winning any horse's trust is important, but with a blind horse it's vital, because they rely so heavily on their riders. You'll have to become his eyes when he can't see, and you need him to trust you to tell him where to go and that it's safe.'

Riding Cassius was everything Kristy hoped it would be and more. She talked to him constantly as they circled the indoor school on both reins, sitting tall in the saddle but making sure she was supple and balanced. He was stiff on his left rein but Emma told her it was nothing regular schooling wouldn't sort out. He was willing and, for his size, surprisingly light on the bit. Kristy wondered how his owner could have ever abandoned him.

As she gazed at his tufty pricked ears Kristy felt a huge wave of responsibility towards Cassius. Physically, he was immensely strong, yet he needed her to look out for him. She decided there and then that she would do whatever it took to gain his trust.

7

EQUESTRIAN BALLET

*K*risty grabbed an apple from the fruit bowl and pulled on her boots.

'Where are you off to so early?' said her mum.

'The stables,' said Kristy in surprise, as if there was anywhere else she'd be going at eight o'clock on a Sunday morning.

'But you don't work on a Sunday. Sunday is homework day.' Her mum, still in her dressing gown, ran a hand through her rumpled hair.

'I won't be long. And I'll do my homework the minute I get in. Promise,' said Kristy, flashing her a smile.

Her mum tutted loudly. 'Those horses see more of you than we do.'

'Oh, Mum, I almost forgot. I got an A for my essay. It was one of the highest marks in the class. And Mr Baker is *really* strict.'

'Good.' Her mum bustled over to the kettle and flicked it on. 'Go on, off you go. I know you can't wait to see those horses of yours. Just make sure you're back in time for lunch.'

'Thanks Mum,' Kristy grinned.

As she reached Mill Farm a car pulled up in front of her and the twins jumped out.

Norah looked her up and down. 'Why are you wearing jodhpurs?'

'Because I'm going riding,' said Kristy evenly.

Norah's eyebrows shot up. 'You're not sneaking another ride, are you?'

'Of course not!' Kristy had no desire to make an enemy of Norah, but she wasn't about to be browbeaten, either. 'Emma wants me to get Cassius fit so she can sell him.'

'The big Percheron in the bottom paddock?' said William, impressed.

Kristy nodded proudly.

'You could have joined us for a ride but we've got a lesson this morning,' said William. 'Maybe next time?'

Kristy pretended not to notice Norah elbowing her brother in the ribs. 'That would be cool. Thanks.'

When Kristy led Cassius up to the yard she was surprised to see Emma tacking up her handsome skewbald gelding, Jigsaw.

'I thought I'd come with you for your first ride. Just to make sure everything's OK.'

Expecting to retrace her steps back down the driveway, Kristy was surprised when Emma turned Jigsaw along the track that led to Cassius's paddock and the back of the farm.

'These lanes are much quieter,' said Emma. They reached a five-bar gate. 'See if you can open it without getting off.'

Kristy spoke quietly to Cassius and turned him side on to the gate. She leant over and he lowered his head so she could reach the latch. She leant further out of the saddle, her arm stretched towards the top bar, but Cassius beat her to it, nudging it open with his nose. Once they were both through he swung his haunches around and backed into the gate until it clicked shut.

'That's some party trick,' laughed Emma.

Kristy grinned and patted the gelding's neck. 'Clever boy!'

They ambled down the lane, past newly-ploughed fields and meadows dotted with dairy cattle and black-faced sheep. Occasionally Cassius would stop, sniff the wind and turn his head so he could see the fields on their right with his good eye. When a tractor pulling a clattering trailer passed them he stood calmly while Jigsaw fidgeted behind him. He didn't even flinch when a pheasant ran squawking out of a holly bush in front of them.

'Good in traffic and bombproof,' said Emma approvingly.

Kristy knew she should be pleased. But it sounded as if her boss was drafting an advert. And her heart plummeted to her boots.

~

KRISTY WAS LIFTING Cassius's saddle onto its rack when Sofia bounced into the tack room. 'Have you got time for a hot chocolate?'

She checked her watch. It was still only half past ten. 'Sure, why not?'

Sofia flicked on the kettle and spooned hot chocolate powder into two mugs. The door to the tack room opened again, this time letting in the twins and a blast of cold air.

'Make us one, too, Sofia,' wheedled William. 'You do it so nicely.'

'Flattery will get you nowhere, William Bergman,' Sofia said sternly. 'Make it yourself.'

William busied himself with mugs and the kettle and gave his sister her drink. Norah, who had bagged the least threadbare armchair, took a tiny sip and pulled a face. 'You forgot my sugar!'

'Sorry, sis.' William handed her a small chipped bowl and

a coffee-stained teaspoon. She eyed him warily. 'Why are you being so nice?'

'Honestly, you're so suspicious.'

'I can't think why.' She tipped two heaped spoonfuls of sugar into her mug and gave it a brisk stir. She sat back in the armchair, cupped her hands around her drink and sighed happily. 'I've been looking forward to this. It's so cold out there.' She took a mouthful, made a strange gurgling noise and spat it straight back into the mug. 'Ugh, salt!'

William's face was a picture of innocence. Norah, on the other hand, had turned an angry shade of puce. 'I hate you!' she shrieked. She leapt from the chair and the mug flew out of her hand, sending a stream of scalding-hot liquid over Kristy, who yelped in pain as the skin on the back of her left hand reddened.

'Now look what you've done!' Norah yelled at her brother. 'Run your hand under the cold tap!' she barked at Kristy. Kristy held her hand under the tap until it had stopped throbbing.

'Is it OK?' William asked sheepishly.

'It's fine.'

'No thanks to you,' said Norah, glaring at her brother. 'She could have suffered third degree burns.'

'What, from a hot chocolate?' William raised his eyebrows.

Kristy, wondering if the twins ever stopped arguing, sank into the sofa and flexed her hand experimentally. The skin was still red but it didn't hurt any more.

Sofia sprang from her chair as if she, too, had been scalded. 'I nearly forgot!' she cried, delving into a plastic carrier bag by her feet. 'Look what I picked up today!' She pulled out a roll of paper with a flourish.

'What is it?' chorused the twins.

'It's a poster for the Mayor's first ever New Year's Eve

show.' Sofia unrolled the poster. 'Look, there'll be ice-skating, a reindeer parade, husky rides and an icicle ball. But most exciting of all, there's going to be a quadrille and,' she paused dramatically, 'they want local riders to enter teams!'

William snorted. 'And how is this exciting?'

Norah rounded on him. 'I bet you don't even know what a quadrille is.'

'It sounds boring, and that's all I need to know.'

'It's a riding display set to music,' said Norah.

'Equestrian ballet,' added Sofia. 'And the riders and their horses have to wear costumes.'

'It still sounds boring,' said William.

'Boring?' Norah exploded. 'It takes great skill to be able to ride in a quadrille.'

'We'll be performing in the town square in front of hundreds of people. How can that be boring?' said Sofia.

Norah frowned. 'We? I thought you wanted us to go and watch.'

Sofia gave an impatient tsk. 'No, silly. We're going to enter a team!'

'No we're not,' said William. 'Riding to music is for girls and sissies.'

'Aha, that's where you're wrong, actually. In the olden days cavalrymen performed quadrilles to prepare their horses for battle. You can't get more heroic than that,' said Sofia.

'I suppose,' said William grudgingly.

Norah's eyes lit up. 'Can I be the team captain?'

'Hey, it was my idea!'

'The team leader needs to be organised, methodical and, most of all, assertive. Sorry Sofia, this job's got my name written all over it,' said Norah.

'You can say that again,' muttered William under his breath.

'If you don't agree to do it I'll tell Mum about you burning Kristy,' said Norah.

'But I didn't -'

'You're already in so much trouble for hiding the car keys in the bread bin.'

'It was meant to be a joke. Alright, I'll do it,' said William, grabbing the poster from Sofia. 'It says the quadrille is open to teams of four.'

'Four?' said Norah. 'But there are only three of us.'

'No there aren't!' cried Sofia. 'What about Kristy?'

Kristy squirmed in her seat as three sets of eyes swivelled in her direction.

8

APOLOGY ACCEPTED

*K*risty hid behind her fringe and plucked at a loose thread on the arm of the sofa.

'But she hasn't got her own pony,' said Norah.

'She can ride Cassius,' said William.

'What, that big old clodhopper?'

'Norah!' cried Sofia, aghast. 'Don't be so mean.'

'I'm just saying what everyone else is thinking,' Norah said huffily.

'Speak for yourself,' said William. 'I think Cassius is cool.'

'If you like woolly mammoths,' said his sister. 'We'd be a laughing stock.'

Kristy could feel a tight bubble of anger building inside her chest. She wasn't bothered that they were talking about her like she wasn't in the room. But there was no way she would let anyone insult Cassius.

'He should be pulling a cart, not riding to music,' Norah continued, not noticing that Kristy had risen to her feet and was glaring at her with flinty eyes.

'Has anyone ever told you you're a bully, Norah Bergman? No, I didn't think so. Let's get one thing straight.

You can be as bossy and rude to me as you like. I can stick up for myself. But don't you ever, *ever*, be mean to Cassius. He's the gentlest, bravest, kindest horse I've ever met. And if you ever looked further than the end of your nose you'd see that. So lay off him, alright?'

Norah looked close to tears and Kristy felt a pang remorse. 'You just need to think before you speak, that's all,' she muttered, pushing past her to the door.

'But will you be in our team?' Sofia called after her.

Kristy stopped in her tracks and swung around to face them. Sofia and William looked hopeful. Norah looked chastened. Kristy shook her head. 'Not in a million years,' she said, slamming the door behind her.

~

EMMA FOUND her in the bottom paddock, watching Cassius graze. She got straight to the point.

'Sofia's said you've had a falling out.'

Kristy was silent.

'I can't have my stablehand arguing with the liveries. What if they decide to take their ponies elsewhere?'

'It was more a difference of opinion,' said Kristy.

'That's not how they described it. But whatever it was, you need to sort it out.'

'You didn't hear them, Emma! Well, just Norah really. She was being so rude about Cassius. She called him a clodhopper!' The Percheron wandered over at the sound of his name and Kristy stroked his nose absentmindedly.

'They told me about this quadrille. They want you to be in their team.'

'They need me to be in their team, more like. There's no-one else,' Kristy said grumpily.

'Don't you think you might actually enjoy it?'

'I like Sofia and William's OK, but Norah treats me like I'm her personal dogsbody. Can you imagine what she'll be like, bossing us all about?'

'I know she can come across as a bit...autocratic -'

'Are you kidding? She's the bossiest person I've ever met.'

'I think it's because she lacks confidence,' said Emma.

Kristy gave her boss an incredulous look.

'No, seriously. Lots of bossy people lack self-esteem. William and Sofia are both naturally talented riders. As are you, if I may say so. But Norah has to work twice as hard to keep up with them. She feels inferior and she disguises it by ordering the others about. She probably doesn't even realise she's doing it.'

'Even if that's true, she's been really unfriendly towards me since I started working here,' said Kristy.

'She probably feels a bit threatened. Worried that you'll steal the others away from her.'

'I'd never do that.'

'I know that, and you know that, but Norah doesn't. Why don't you prove it to her?'

Kristy picked a handful of grass and offered it to Cassius. 'How?'

'By joining their team. And Cassius would love it.'

'That's blackmail,' Kristy sighed.

Cassius gave her a gentle nudge, as if he agreed with Emma.

'Where's your fighting spirit? Prove her wrong. Show her that he isn't a clodhopper,' Emma persisted.

Kristy felt outnumbered. 'All right, I'll think about it. On one condition. She needs to apologise first.'

≈

KRISTY WAS SITTING in her usual spot in the library the next day, finishing a history assignment, when someone cleared their throat and said nervously, 'Have you got a minute?'

She swung around to see Norah standing behind her, clutching her schoolbag to her chest, her face solemn.

'That depends,' said Kristy slowly, 'on what you've come to say.'

Norah took a deep breath. 'I'm sorry I spilled my drink over your hand. I'm sorry I was rude to you. But most of all I'm sorry I was mean about Cassius. He's not a clodhopper. I don't even know why I said it. William's always telling me I'm a bigmouth and he's right.'

'Shhh!' hissed the librarian, pointing to a sign hanging over the door. *Quiet please.*

'Sorry,' mouthed Norah to the librarian, sliding into the chair next to Kristy. She grinned self-consciously and whispered, 'I seem to be doing a lot of apologising today.'

Kristy put her pen down carefully.

'Please be in the team, Kristy. We need you.'

'That depends,' said Kristy.

'On what? I'll do anything.'

'I totally get that you can treat me like your personal slave when I'm working. But you have to give me your word that when we're training for the quadrille we're equals. No ordering me about like I'm the hired help, OK?'

'I wouldn't dream of it,' said Norah earnestly. 'If it'll make a difference I've told Sofia she should be the leader. After all, it was her idea.'

Kristy raised her eyebrows. 'Yes, it was.'

'We're having a meeting to discuss it all in the tack room at six o'clock tonight. We've made it then so you'll have finished your shift. Please say you'll come?' She looked at Kristy with anxious eyes.

Kristy had enjoyed watching the other girl squirm but she wasn't one to hold a grudge. 'Apology accepted.' She gathered her books, shoved them into her bag and stood up. 'Alright, I'll come.'

≈

A CHINK of golden light slunk through a knot in the wooden door of the tack room like a solitary ray of sunshine as Kristy walked past, pushing the final wheelbarrow-load of clean straw to Copper's stable. The chestnut gelding was tied up outside, his head buried in a haynet, snug in his quilted rug. As Sofia, Norah and William had all ridden tonight Kristy hadn't had to bring the ponies in or change their rugs. She was almost finished and it was still only a quarter to six.

Emma followed her into Copper's stable and took the fork from Kristy's hand.

'I'll finish off here. You go and have your powwow.'

Kristy pushed open the tack room door.

'You're here!' cried Sofia with relief.

Kristy kicked off her muddy boots and curled up in an armchair.

'Can I make you a hot chocolate?' asked Norah.

'As long as you don't throw it over me this time,' Kristy deadpanned.

Sofia giggled and reached for a notebook. She waved it at them. 'I've written an agenda for the meeting -'

'Crikey, that's a bit official, isn't it? This is supposed to be fun, remember,' William grumbled.

Ignoring him, Sofia continued, 'It was Norah's idea. It's so I don't forget anything. You know what I'm like.'

Norah smiled proudly. William muttered something under his breath.

'The first thing we need to decide is who's going to be in charge of what. I'm talking routine, music, costumes, that kind of thing.'

'I'll be in charge of the routine. I've been researching quadrilles and have some ideas already,' said Norah.

'OK, we'll take a vote on that,' said Sofia. 'Everyone in favour, raise your hands. Good. A unanimous decision. Who wants to look after the costumes?'

'I don't mind,' said Kristy.

'Don't forget we need costumes for the horses too,' said Norah. 'It's a lot of work. Are you sure you've got time?'

'Yeah, it'll be fine.'

'I can help. I'm a dab hand with a needle,' said Sofia. 'All in favour? Great. Just the music to decide now.'

'Looks like that's down to me,' said William.

'Agreed?' asked Sofia.

'Agreed,' they chorused back.

'Awesome. We'll meet again on Friday night. Bring along your initial ideas and we'll start training sessions next week. That gives us just over a month until the show.'

'It's not long, is it?' said Kristy. 'Cassius isn't as fit as your ponies, remember.'

'It'll be fine,' said Sofia, flicking her notebook shut. 'What can possibly go wrong?'

9

EARLY BIRD

*T*he shrill sound of Kristy's alarm dragged her from a dreamless sleep. She forced her eyes open and stared blearily at the luminous-green clock dial and groaned. It was six o'clock. Waking up at the crack of dawn to exercise Cassius before school had seemed like a good idea the previous day, although her parents had taken some convincing. Now an extra hour's sleep seemed infinitely more inviting.

Kristy flung her duvet off before she could change her mind. She needed to be at the stables by half past six if she was to be back in time for school. To her surprise her dad was dressed and sitting at the breakfast bar sipping a cup of coffee when she pushed open the kitchen door.

'Your mum bet me you wouldn't get up. I said you would. And I was right,' he smiled. 'Grab your coat. I'll run you to the stables.'

'Thanks Dad!'

'My pleasure. I've been wanting to meet Cassius anyway. You know my grandfather used to have two Percherons on his farm?'

'You never told me that.'

Her dad's eyes took on a faraway look. 'I used to ride them while they were pulling the plough. One was grey and the other black. They were called Salt and Pepper.'

When Kristy's dad saw Cassius, he did a double take. 'Incredible. He looks just like Pepper. You're right, he's beautiful, Kristy. And I love the way he tilts his head to watch us.'

Kristy felt an unpleasant flutter in her stomach. When she'd told her parents about Cassius she had omitted to add that the Percheron had lost the sight in one eye. Her mum was a terrible worrier. If she even had an inkling that Kristy was riding a half-blind horse she'd put a stop to it, no question. She risked a look at her dad. He was running a hand down Cassius's neck while the gelding nuzzled him.

'You're a natural with him,' she said, surprised.

'I told you, I virtually grew up with Grandpa's horses.' He looked closely at Cassius's cloudy eye and then waved a hand back and forth in front of it. Cassius didn't flinch. 'That's odd,' he said to himself.

'He's blind in that eye,' Kristy blurted. 'I should have told you, I know, but I didn't want Mum to fret. You know what she's like.'

'I do, but Kristy -'

'He's adapted really well,' Kristy said, hopping from one foot to the other. 'He can see perfectly out of his left eye and when we're out I act as his eyes. He looks after me and I look after him.'

Her dad nodded slowly, and looked Cassius in his good eye. 'You'll keep her safe, my old friend? I've grown quite fond of her over the years.'

'*Dad!*' Kristy rolled her eyes.

'OK. Here's the deal. I'll stay to watch you ride. If I think he's safe then fine, you can carry on as before and we won't worry your mother. But if not, I'll have to tell her, Kristy. And I know what she'll say.'

So did Kristy. As she slipped on the gelding's bridle she whispered in his ear, 'We need to be the best we can be, Cassius. Otherwise it's game over. You, me, the team. Everything. And we can't let that happen, OK?'

As Kristy led Cassius over to the mounting block she could feel her heart beating twice as fast as normal. She tightened his girth and ran down the stirrups, trying to breathe steadily and slow her heart rate. The last thing she needed was for the Percheron to pick up on her butterflies. He stood as still as granite as she climbed the mounting block and sprang lightly into the saddle. She patted his neck, took a deep breath and inclined her head towards the indoor school. 'It's this way.'

Kristy kept up her usual steady stream of chatter as Cassius walked around the ring on the left rein, flexing his powerful neck. When she asked him for a trot he obliged willingly, and she grinned as she settled into the rhythmic two-time beat. She kicked him into a canter and sat down to his rocking horse stride for half a length of the school until she could sense he was starting to tire.

When her dad sneezed explosively Kristy felt Cassius's muscles tense beneath her.

'It's alright,' she soothed. 'It just Dad's dust allergy.' The Percheron gave a tiny shake of his head and trotted on, his big hooves carving crescents in the sand surface of the indoor school.

'Sorry,' her dad said as they trotted past. 'I'll take an anti-histamine next time I come.'

Kristy felt a smile creep onto her face. As Cassius loped around the ring she felt as though she was floating on air. They'd passed her dad's test. There would be a next time.

~

As THEY DROVE home Kristy told her dad about the quadrille.

'It sounds like a lot of fun,' he said.

'I'm responsible for costumes, but I've no idea what to do.'

'It's a winter show, so what about a winter theme?'

'Are you saying we should all dress up as Christmas trees?' Kristy giggled, imagining the scene of devastation if greedy Silver started nibbling their costumes.

'Not Christmas trees necessarily. What about Christmas angels?'

'William would have a meltdown. He's already worried his friends at school will call him a sissy. And don't forget that the horses have to have costumes, too.'

'OK, so no angels or Christmas trees.' Kristy's dad ran a hand through his hair as he thought. 'Icicles?'

'Too pointy.'

'Christmas elves?'

Kristy pulled a face.

He banged the palm of his hand on the steering wheel. 'I've got it! You can dress as snowmen!'

Kristy was about to pour scorn on the idea, but then an image of the four of them dressed as snowmen as they cantered into the ring popped into her head. They would look awesome.

'We could wear white onesies with black pompoms sewn on for buttons and paint our faces white. I could easily make cardboard carrots for noses and turn our riding hats into top hats. We can wear scarves and the horses can wear white sheets. It's a great idea, Dad.'

He pulled in outside their apartment block and smiled. 'My pleasure.'

10

WOODEN HORSES

'Welcome to the second meeting of the Mill Farm Stables quadrille team,' said Norah. She stood up and handed them each a plastic folder, pink for the girls, blue for William.

'I thought Sofia was supposed to be team captain,' grumbled William, peering at her over the top of his mobile phone.

'No phones during quadrille meetings. You know the rules,' Norah barked.

'Rules?' he spluttered.

Ignoring him, Norah opened her own folder. 'Inside is our five-minute routine. I have tried to keep it simple, so although there are changes of rein, serpentines and two-way crossovers, it will all be done at a trot. I thought cantering and flying changes might be a bit ambitious for some of us.'

Kristy didn't like the way Norah looked at her as she said this, but decided to let it go.

'I've been reading up on quadrilles. Marks are usually awarded for turnout, content of the programme and general artistic impression. It doesn't matter if the horses and ponies aren't the same size or colour, they just need to be in time with each other. Clear so far?'

Kristy and Sofia nodded. William yawned loudly.

'One member of the team needs to be the leader and dictate speed. That'll be me, obviously, as you voted unanimously for me to take charge of the routine.' Norah smiled benevolently at them all.

'Obviously,' said Kristy, noticing William's mouth twitch.

'We ride at the pace of the slowest pony -'

'Silver,' supplied William.

Norah's eyes flashed dangerously.

Sofia glanced from one twin to the other. 'It's not a race, guys.'

'You're right,' said Norah, narrowing her eyes at her brother. 'It's important the bigger horses, like Cassius, keep pace with the slower ones, whoever they may be. So, you might have to collect him at the trot, Kristy.'

'No problem,' Kristy shrugged nonchalantly, even though she knew as much about collection as she did about piaffes and pirouettes, which was not much.

'In your folder you will find the routine, along with plans of some of the moves you might not have come across, such as threading the needle.'

'Hey, I thought Kristy was doing the costumes,' joked William.

'Threading the needle is where horses coming from opposite sides of the arena cross over on the diagonal. You think they're going to crash, but they pass between each other. If you look, I've drawn a diagram on appendix B.'

Kristy shuffled her papers to find the page Norah was pointing at. It was a confusing mass of lines, arrows, boxes and numbers.

'Each of us have a number. I'm one, Sofia is two, William is three and Kristy is four.'

The more Kristy stared at the page the more bewildered she became.

'You're holding it upside down,' said Norah helpfully.

Kristy felt a flush creep up her neck. But when she glanced at Sofia, the older girl looked as baffled as she was.

'So, for your homework -'

'*Homework?*' cried William, aghast.

'For your homework, I want you all to memorise the routine and we'll have a run-through after Kristy's finished work tomorrow.'

'With the horses?' Kristy asked faintly, thinking, *it'll be carnage*.

'Of course not!' Norah scoffed. 'We need to nail it ourselves before we start riding it. We'll just walk it through until I'm satisfied you know what you're supposed to be doing.'

Sofia stood up and smiled weakly. 'Right, that's the routine sorted. Next on the agenda is the music. William, have you made any headway?'

William switched his attention from the game he was playing on his mobile. 'Ah well,' he said, 'I thought I needed to see the routine before I chose the music, otherwise it might not fit.'

'In other words he hasn't done it yet,' said Norah under her breath.

'Good point, William,' said Sofia. 'Kristy, what about costumes?'

Kristy reached in the carrier bag at her feet for her sketchpad. She'd spent the previous evening jotting down ideas and sketching outlines of how their snowmen costumes would look.

She licked her lips and passed the sketchbook to Sofia. 'I thought we could go as snowmen. It ties in nicely with the winter theme and although it's pretty straightforward it should look really eye-catching. I've found some white onesies online. They're not expensive. I'll do the carrots and buttons and hats and stuff. We can buy matching scarves really cheaply. And everyone has a spare white sheet lurking at the back of the airing cupboard.'

Sofia nodded and passed the sketchbook to the twins. 'Excellent idea. It gets my vote.'

'Abominable snowmen would have been way cooler. Yeti rock,' said William, glancing at Kristy's drawings. 'But snowmen are fine with me.'

All eyes turned to Norah. On paper she may have only been in charge of the routine, but everyone knew deep down that she was their leader. If she didn't like Kristy's costumes it would be back to the drawing board. And time was running out.

She studied the sketches carefully, her eyebrows scrunched into question marks. Kristy realised she was holding her breath.

'You don't like them, do you?' she said, resigned.

'I don't like them, no,' Norah agreed. She handed the drawings back to Kristy and her face broke into a smile. 'I love them!'

NORAH TAPPED a riding crop against her thigh impatiently.

'Come on, you lot. We've only got the indoor school for half an hour.'

'Why are you holding a crop?' said Sofia nervously.

Norah looked at Sofia as if she was stupid. 'So I can point out where you're supposed to be going.'

'I reckon it's to beat us with if we don't do as we're told,' William whispered to Kristy. She stifled a giggle.

Norah narrowed her eyes at her brother. 'Perhaps you'd like to share your joke with the rest of the team?'

William stared at his boots. 'Probably not.'

'Don't forget, I'm number one, Sofia's number two, William's number three and Kristy, you're number four. Line up behind me in order and we'll walk up the centre line and peel off at A, me and Sofia to the left and William and Kristy to the right.'

Kristy shuffled self-consciously behind the others and at the far end followed William as he walked down the length of the school.

'So, at the bottom turn towards the centre line again, but this time pair up with your opposite number. That's me and William, and Sofia and Kristy,' said Norah.

'Having fun?' asked Sofia as she drew level with Kristy.

'I feel ridiculous,' Kristy hissed out of the corner of her mouth. 'Good job no-one's watching.'

'We're going to ride a three-loop serpentine and drop back into single file at A,' yelled Norah.

'Which one's A?' cried Kristy in panic.

Sofia pointed at the entrance. 'Where we came in.'

As they walked along the length of the school Norah waved her crop at them. 'This is one of the more complex moves, so pay attention. When I hit M we all turn left together and walk across the school four abreast. Then, when we reach the other side, we turn right and fall back into single file on the right rein.'

Kristy followed William, trying not to tread on his heels, and wondered if she would ever remember the routine. It seemed hideously complicated.

'Now we trot around the school to E and do a twenty metre circle on the right rein leading into a figure of eight. Then at C we do another twenty metre circle on the left rein followed by another figure of eight back to A. All clear so far?'

'As clear as mud,' William muttered.

Kristy could tell Norah was in her element, bossing them around. 'Another tricky move coming up. At A we turn right up the centre line and when I reach H we all turn into 10 metre circles on the left rein, ride back up the centre line for a few strides and then do 10 metres circles on the right rein. Got it?'

Sofia was biting her bottom lip in concentration. 'Yes, I've got it! Clever,' she nodded approvingly. Norah glowed.

They walked back up the centre line. Kristy tried to imagine Cassius's pricked ears in front of her. 'It's quite a long routine,' she said.

'We're nearly finished,' Norah panted. 'And we'll be doing it all at a trot, don't forget. I haven't timed it, but I reckon it'll take five minutes. Now for the showpiece. Folks, we are about to thread the needle! William, you follow me onto the left rein again, and Kristy, follow Sofia onto the right. We cross over at X. Me first, then Sofia, then William and finally Kristy. That's why I've put you last, Kristy - so you can stay out of trouble at the back. If Cassius collided with one of the other ponies we'd be in serious trouble!' Norah gave a little tinkle of laughter. Kristy smiled through gritted teeth.

'Then we ride in our pairs up the centre line and all line up in front of the judges, giving a salute like so.' Norah demonstrated by holding imaginary reins in her left hand, dropping her right hand to her side and nodding. She glanced at her watch. 'We've got time for one more run-through, but this time we'll do it at a trot, I mean jog.'

The others groaned. Norah fixed them all with a steely glare. 'Practice makes perfect. You don't want to make a spectacle of yourselves in front of the whole town, do you?'

'I suppose not,' Sofia conceded. 'But isn't there a way we

can make it a bit more realistic? I feel stupid just walking around.'

William chuckled to himself. 'I have just the thing, ladies. Wait there, I'll be right back.'

'Brooms?' cried Norah, when her brother reappeared minutes later dragging four of Emma's yard brooms behind him.

'That's where you're wrong, sister dear. These are not brooms, they are our wooden steeds, come to help us practice our routine until we're safe enough to be let loose on the real thing.'

Kristy made a beeline for her favourite yard broom and pretended to swing into the saddle. 'Come on, Norah. It'll be fun.' She clicked her tongue and galloped the broom in a loop. 'Look,' she cried. 'A perfect ten metre circle!'

Sofia took a broom, sprung into the saddle and trotted serenely behind Kristy.

When William jumped on a third broom and began careering down the side of the indoor like a rodeo rider, shouting yee-haw at regular intervals, Norah knew she was beaten.

Sighing, she picked up the last broom and called them back to order. 'Alright, no more high jinks. We need to concentrate on the routine. Remember to keep even spaces between your broom and the broom in front.'

It was much more fun following the moves on their imaginary horses. Even Norah saw the funny side when William's broom clipped Sofia's during the threading the needle and they both collapsed on the ground in hysterics. They were having so much fun that they decided to run through the routine a third and final time, and by the time they stopped in front of the judge they were all rosy-cheeked and breathless.

'Bravo!' called Emma from the entrance to the indoor school.

Norah groaned. 'No-one's going to take me seriously ever again.'

'No offence, but you need to lighten up, sis,' said her brother. 'It's supposed to be fun, remember.'

～

THAT NIGHT KRISTY dreamt it was the day of the show and they were riding their routine in the town square, watched by hundreds of people. Cassius looked as if he was going into battle with his neck proudly arched and his white sheet like a medieval caparison. He floated into the square in a beautifully collected trot and the crowds clapped and cheered. Kristy felt her heart swell with love for the big, brave Percheron. But as they swept through their serpentine people started laughing and pointing at them. The babble of laughter grew louder and Kristy looked around her wildly, wondering what was causing such hilarity.

'Couldn't she afford a proper horse?' cried a small boy.

Kristy looked down and to her horror Cassius had disappeared and she was riding a wooden broom. But this broom had a life of its own, leaping and prancing like a wild mustang. She tried to control it but it was impossible. The broom kept twisting and bucking. Feeling herself slipping, she gripped the broom handle so tightly her knuckles went white. But it was no good. When the broom finally went into a ninety degree spin she was thrown to the floor, landing unceremoniously on her backside. Kristy howled with pain and the crowds howled with laughter. The broom cavorted out of the square and Norah cantered over on Silver and skidded to a halt centimetres from Kristy. Her eyes blazing, Norah shouted, 'I *knew* we should have asked someone else to join the team. You're a disaster, Kristy Moore. You and that blind old clodhopper have ruined *everything*!'

Kristy jolted awake, her heart racing. The dream had felt so real she could still feel the flush of embarrassment burning her cheeks. She knew Norah thought she and Cassius were the weak links in the team. As she lay in bed staring at the ceiling, Kristy vowed to do whatever it took to prove her wrong.

PRIVATE LESSONS

*K*risty sat at the breakfast bar the following morning surrounded by pieces of paper. As she dipped a spoon absentmindedly into her bowl of porridge she studied Norah's routine, her brows knotted in concentration as she visualised the moves. Once she'd finished her porridge she drew the routine over and over again, muttering under her breath as she did, 'Right at C, serpentine, twenty metre circle, figure of eight. Don't get too close to Copper! Don't forget the salute!'

'Homework?' smiled her mum, flicking on the kettle and spooning coffee into two mugs.

Kristy tried not to look guilty. She should have been doing her homework. She had a history assignment to write. But that could wait. The quadrille was more important.

'Kind of,' she said, gathering the papers before her mum could see.

'You've got your jodhpurs on. You're not going to the stables *again?*'

'Just for a couple of hours. It's really important I get Cassius fit, Mum.'

Her mum sighed. 'I know. Dad told me about the quadrille. I'd like to come and watch you ride. I could pop over this morning if you like?'

'This morning?' said Kristy, her voice rising an octave.

Her mum gave her a wounded look. 'Don't you want me to?'

Kristy knew that if her mum found out that Cassius was blind in one eye she would never be allowed to ride him again. It was vital that she didn't go anywhere near Mill Farm until after the quadrille.

'Of course I want you to. But we've only just started practising. I want you to see us when we're polished and professional. So you can be really proud of me,' Kristy added with a hopeful smile.

'OK, we'll save it for the show. But take Dad's camera and get some nice photos of Cassius. I'd like to know what he looks like.'

~

KRISTY SWEPT the dandy brush over Cassius's thick winter coat. Her early morning rides were doing the job - he already looked fitter and his muscle tone had improved. He lifted each leg so Kristy could pick out his feet, and nibbled her pockets while she combed his long, wavy mane.

'I've learnt the routine and we're going to have a go at it, just the two of us,' Kristy told him. 'We'll try it at a walk first, and then at a trot. But I don't want you turning into a broom halfway around, OK?' she said, rubbing his ear.

Although he didn't turn into a broom, their serpentine was woefully wonky and their figure of eights left a lot to be desired. Kristy found it hard to judge the size of a twenty metre circle and the ten metre circles seemed impossibly small for a horse as big as Cassius. She had no idea how they would manage one in a trot. 'But it gives us a good foundation on which to build,' she told the gelding, more confidently than she felt.

She walked him around the school on a long rein so he could stretch his neck before they attempted the routine in a trot. Remembering the moves was even harder when they came around so much faster, and she forgot the two twenty metre circles completely.

Perhaps Norah was right, she thought gloomily. Perhaps they were the weak link in the team. She'd once crept in to watch Sofia schooling Jazz, and the older girl had made leg yields, half-passes and flying changes look easy. Compared to her, they were complete amateurs.

Kristy gathered her reins. 'One more go and then we're done, I promise.'

Once more Cassius trotted willingly around the school. If he wondered why his young rider kept changing her mind as she steered him this way and that, muddling her aids, he didn't protest. He just carried on, as steady as a rock. Kristy knew not every horse would be so obliging.

Emma was in the yard. 'How did it go?'

'Not great,' Kristy admitted. 'But that was down to me, not Cassius. He didn't put a foot wrong.'

'Have you done any dressage before?'

She shook her head.

'Would you like me to give you some lessons?'

Kristy's jaw dropped. 'You said riding wasn't part of the job.'

'I'm doing it because it suits me. I'm much more likely to sell Cassius if you've been schooling him.'

Kristy bit her lip. She'd pushed the fact that Emma still planned to sell Cassius to the very back of her mind. She jumped off and busied herself loosening his girth and running up her stirrup leathers while she considered the offer. If she said yes, someone was likely to snap Cassius up when Emma advertised him. Yet she knew they needed to practice more if they weren't going to let down the team. It was a horrible dilemma.

'Well?' said Emma.

Kristy played with a hank of Cassius's mane. 'Yes please,' she said eventually.

Emma clapped her hands. 'Excellent. We'll start at six thirty tomorrow.'

~

'WE'LL BEGIN with some simple circles and figures of eight,' said Emma, as she stood in the centre of the school and watched Kristy appraisingly.

'Shouldn't we just work on the routine?' said Kristy.

'Definitely not. If you ride the whole thing too often Cassius will learn it, too, and will start to anticipate the movements, and we don't want that. We'll practice it in sections, so you are comfortable with all the movements, before we put it all together. Right, I'd like you to change rein diagonally from F to H.'

As they passed F Kristy tugged the Percheron's left rein and squeezed with her right leg.

'Look in the direction you want to turn. Check his inside rein lightly to warn him you are about to ask him to turn, and then open your inside rein. Make sure your inside leg is on the girth and your outside leg is just behind so he keeps his momentum. You want him to bend his whole body, not just his neck. Try again at H.'

Kristy ran through Emma's instructions in her head. *Look where you want to go. Lightly check with the inside rein. Open the inside rein. Inside leg on the girth. Outside leg just behind.*

'Much better,' said Emma. 'But you need to relax your

arms more and sit up tall in the saddle. No, you've hollowed your back now. Imagine there's a line running from your shoulder through your hip, down to your heel. That's it, well done. Now we'll try a figure of eight.'

'How do I make my circles circle-shaped and not egg-shaped?' Kristy asked desperately as Cassius drifted onto his forehand.

'Look where you're going. That's really important. Make sure he's flexing in the direction of the bend. You should just be able to see his eye. And keep your outside leg slightly back so he doesn't swing his quarters out and turn your lovely circle into an oblong.'

'It's a lot to remember.'

Emma laughed. 'We haven't tried it at a trot yet!'

The next morning they tackled a serpentine. Kristy gazed at the school, trying to work out her line.

'Don't over-complicate it,' said Emma. 'It's just a series of semi-circles with a change of rein every time you cross the centre line. Just make sure each loop is equal in size and shape.'

'So if I start at C on the right rein I turn at M, E and F?'

'That's right. Make sure Cassius is bent around your inside leg and as you change rein over the centre line ride in a straight line for a few strides before you ask him to bend in the opposite direction.'

Cassius's stiffness on his left rein was more pronounced as they walked the serpentine.

'Don't worry. That should improve in time. He hasn't been schooled for well over a year, don't forget. I'd say he's doing pretty well,' said Emma.

Kristy allowed herself a small smile, even though there wasn't a bone in her body that didn't ache. The early morning riding lessons and the two hours of mucking out after school were beginning to take their toll and she was permanently exhausted. The previous lunchtime she had even fallen asleep over her books as she'd sat in the library, and had woken, dry-mouthed and dazed, when the bell for lessons had sounded. She was constantly stifling yawns at home and was in bed and fast asleep by a quarter past eight most nights. If her parents had any inkling how shattered she was they would ban her from the stables, no question.

Kristy was also terrified her school grades were in danger of slipping. She was running through the quadrille in her head when she should have been concentrating in lessons and she was rushing her homework. Although Mr Baker had been pleased with her essay on Percherons, he'd only given her a C for her latest assignment. Kristy didn't blame him. She'd dashed it off in about ten minutes flat during morning break.

' - Kristy, I said left rein, not right!'

Brought swiftly back to the present by the ring of exasperation in Emma's voice, Kristy dipped her head. 'Sorry,' she muttered.

'Alright, but you need to concentrate. Otherwise we may as well not bother.'

Kristy banished all other thoughts from her head as she focused on the rest of the lesson, and at the end Emma patted her on the back and said 'Good job'.

But it was little consolation and as her dad drove her home she stared glumly out of the window, answering in monosyllables when he asked her about her lesson. Through the steamed-up windows the streets were as dank and grey as her mood. The problem was inescapable. When she was at the stables she worried about school, and when she was at school all she could think about was Cassius and the quadrille. Something had to change. Kristy just didn't know what.

12

A HELPING HAND

Kristy's heart sank when she saw Norah making a beeline for her at morning break the following day. It plummeted even further when she recognised the determined jut of Norah's jaw as she clasped a clipboard to her chest and forced her way through a swarm of schoolchildren all heading in the opposite direction.

'Kristy!' she said, her smile not quite reaching her eyes. 'I'm glad I've found you. I just wanted to see where we were with the costumes.'

If Kristy had thought her heart couldn't have sunk any lower, she was wrong.

'The thing is, Norah,' she said, 'I've been a bit busy. I haven't actually made a start on them yet.'

'Oh,' said Norah, writing something on her clipboard. 'That's a bit of a worry. We only have just over three weeks before the show, you know.'

'I do know,' Kristy said evenly. 'And they will get done. I'll bring a tape measure tonight and get everyone's measurements so I can order the onesies. Have you found white sheets for Silver and Copper yet?' she asked, hoping to wrong-foot her.

Norah smiled complacently. 'Yes, all sorted. Mum bought new ones, actually.'

'Excellent. At least that's one thing you can tick off your checklist, hey?'

Kristy was inordinately pleased to see a dull flush creep up Norah's neck. 'I'll see you tonight. After I've mucked out your pony. And soaked his hay,' she added, plunging into the mass of children without a backward glance.

~

Kristy was still basking in her tiny victory when Sofia found her in the library at lunch. They'd fallen into an easy routine, catching up in snatched whispers for ten minutes before settling down companionably, Sofia reading whatever pony book she was currently devouring, and Kristy working her way through her piles of homework.

'You're looking very pleased with yourself,' said Sofia.

'I saw Norah at break. She was hounding me about the costumes. I reminded her that I've got a little bit more on my plate than she has, what with working all hours and getting Cassius fit. I think she got the message.'

'Good. She can be a bit bossy, I know -'

'You can say that again,' said Kristy.

'- but she means well.'

'What I don't understand is how she suddenly seems to be in charge. You were supposed to be our leader. It's like she's taken over by stealth.'

'I know,' Sofia sighed. 'But she's so much better at it than me.'

Kristy looked at her pile of books in despair.

'What's up?'

'I literally don't know where to start. Every teacher is handing out homework like it's going out of fashion. And if my grades drop I'll have to stop working at Mill Farm. And if that happens I won't be able to ride Cassius. And if I can't ride Cassius I'll have to drop out of the team.'

Sofia looked at Kristy in horror. 'We can't let that happen!'

'Believe me, it's the last thing I want, too. But I'm struggling to fit it all in.'

'I'll help you with the costumes for a start,' said Sofia decisively. 'How else can we help?'

Kristy gave her friend a wan smile. 'You could do my history assignment for me. It's supposed to be in tomorrow and I haven't even started it.'

Sofia stared into the distance. 'I've got an even better idea,' she finally announced. 'Leave it with me.'

⁓

WHEN KRISTY ARRIVED at the stables just before four o'clock she was surprised to see Sofia and the twins already there.

'You're early,' she said.

'There's a reason for that,' Sofia grinned. 'We're here to help.'

'What do you mean?'

'Sofia said you were struggling to fit everything in,' said Norah, giving Kristy a faintly patronising look as if she would never have been so feeble. 'She suggested that if we helped muck out you'd be finished in an hour and we can bring our quadrille meeting forward so you can go home early and do your homework.'

Kristy fiddled with the zip of her coat. 'Emma won't like it. She's paying me to work.'

'We've cleared it with her,' said William. 'She said she didn't mind who did the jobs as long as they were done.'

'And it's only while we're training for the quadrille,' said Norah. 'After that you won't need us, will you?'

'But Sofia, you said your dad would go mad if he found out he was paying for work you were doing.'

Sofia waved a hand dismissively. 'I'm not going to tell him, are you?'

Kristy looked at them all in turn. 'It's very kind of you, and I really appreciate it, but I can't let you help. I can cope.' She set off towards the barn but Norah stepped into her path.

'I wasn't sure it was a good idea at first, either. I wondered why we should do the work you're being paid to do. But I'm not doing this for you, Kristy, I'm doing it for the team. So just accept our help with good grace and move on. Alright?'

Norah's eyes burned with intensity, but there was no animosity there. Kristy realised that although she might not always like what the other girl had to say, at least she spoke her mind. Perhaps Sofia was right and Norah did mean well. And if she was able to go home early she would have time to finish the two assignments due in the morning. Otherwise she would be setting the alarm for five o'clock.

She knew that if she didn't change something there was a chance she would crack under the strain. And here was a solution, being offered to her on a plate.

'For the team?' she said.

'For the team,' Norah repeated.

Kristy smiled gratefully. 'Thank you.'

They worked quickly, Sofia, William and Norah mucking out their own ponies while Kristy ran around emptying wheelbarrows, laying down fresh straw and filling haynets and water buckets. It took a quarter of the time it normally took her.

When Kristy said as much, Norah rolled her eyes. 'Well, it would, wouldn't it? There are four times as many people. Do you need some help with your maths, too?'

Instead of taking offence, as she would normally do, Kristy teased, 'Come to mention it, I have got a maths worksheet that needs finishing if you're offering?'

Norah forked the last of Silver's wet bedding into the wheelbarrow. 'Very funny. Now go and empty that barrow, please, or I might change my mind about helping.'

By five past five the three ponies were tucked up in their stables. Kristy had even had ten minutes to groom Cassius. And, if the quadrille practice went well, she should be home before six.

She found the others in the tack room. William was fiddling with his mobile phone. 'I've chosen the music. We wanted something with a good beat, something the horses could trot in time to, right?'

'Yes,' said Norah impatiently.

'Here we go.' William touched the screen and sat back, his arms linked behind his head and a roguish look in his eye. Kristy jumped out of her skin when the sound of a distorted electric guitar tore through the quiet tack room like the amplified and unearthly shriek of a barn owl. A loud drum and base beat morphed into an aggressive guitar solo. It was so loud Kristy covered her ears.

Norah sprang to her feet, snatched her brother's phone and, much to Kristy's relief, turned the volume down.

'Have you gone totally mad?' she squawked.

'Why not? Don't you like heavy metal?' he asked innocently.

'We can't do dressage to that kind of music, you idiot! It'll frighten the horses out of their wits. I can't trust you with anything, can I? What were you thinking?'

But William had collapsed into fits of giggles. 'It was a joke,' he spluttered. 'Of course that's not the music. I had you all going for a while, though, didn't I?'

Norah lunged for her brother but he held up his hands in mock surrender. 'OK, I'm sorry. If you give me back my phone I'll play the real music.'

She slammed it into the palm of his hand and hissed, 'It had better be good.'

This time the mellow sound of a cello was the cue for a classical piece of music Kristy recognised but couldn't name. She was pretty sure it had been used in a film. Far from being stuffy, it was uplifting and fun, and she was soon tapping her toes in time to its beat. She glanced at the others. Norah was sitting with her eyes closed, her head nodding imperceptibly. Sofia was drumming her hands on her thighs, a wide smile on her face. William was looking smug.

When the music ended, William switched his mobile off. 'Well?' he said.

'Much better,' said Norah.

'I loved it,' said Kristy.

'Me too,' added Sofia.

'That's good, because we'll be sick of hearing it by New Year's,' William said.

'Oh, I nearly forgot!' cried Sofia. She fished around in a carrier bag at her feet and produced four large balls of black wool and a number of small cardboard discs, each with a round hole in the middle.

'To help Kristy out with the costumes, we've each got to make our own pom poms for our buttons,' she said, handing out the discs and wool.

'I don't know how to make a pom pom,' said William. 'Isn't it enough that I found us some awesome music?'

'No,' said Sofia firmly. 'We all need to do our share. Norah'll show you. They're ever so easy.'

Kristy looked at Sofia gratefully. 'How did you manage to find all that wool so quickly?'

'Mum's always knitting and she's got stacks of the stuff at home. I'll help you sew them on and make the hats and carrots.'

Kristy held the wool to her cheek. It was silky soft and reminded her of Cassius's thick winter coat. She sat cross-legged on the sofa watching the twins play-fighting and Sofia humming along to William's music.

For the first time since she'd moved, Kristy felt as though she belonged somewhere. She knew she was probably being fanciful, but she could picture roots as strong as an oak tree's binding her to Mill Farm Stables, Cassius and her three new friends. And it felt good.

13

BLIND SPOT

*A*fter a week practising the routine on their brooms, Norah felt they were ready to run through some of the moves on the horses. Even though Kristy's lessons with Emma had been going well, and her serpentines and figures of eight were actually beginning to resemble the movements they were supposed to be and not the random scribbles of a hyperactive toddler, she still felt unaccountably nervous.

She was at the stables early, having decided that if she was going to make a show of herself, it might as well be on a beautifully turned-out horse.

Cassius heard the gate click open and tilted his head to watch her. It was a trait of his that melted her heart, making her feel fierce, sad and proud all at the same time. She called him softly and he ambled over and gave her a friendly nudge.

Kristy spent the next hour grooming the Percheron until this thick winter coat shone. She oiled his hooves and sponged his face. She even gave his saddle and bridle a quick polish before she tacked him up and followed William and Copper into the school.

The chestnut gelding had a long, loping gait and matched

the big Percheron stride for stride. At the top end of the school William followed his sister and Kristy peeled off behind Sofia and Jazz. Jazz was hopelessly over-excited and Kristy checked Cassius, trying to keep him as far as possible from her skittering hooves.

Sofia turned around. 'It's OK, she doesn't kick.'

Kristy nodded but still kept a healthy distance. If Jazz did lash out on Cassius's blind side who knew how much damage she would cause. They paired up at the bottom of the school, Norah with Sofia, William with Kristy.

'Serpentine!' Norah barked, leading them through a passable serpentine before they filed in behind each other again. Norah eased Silver into a walk at M and the others followed suit, changing rein and picking up a trot.

Kristy was beginning to enjoy herself. Despite the fact that Cassius was far less fit than the ponies, he was maintaining a good working trot without getting too puffed out. Jazz seemed to have finally settled and they completed their two ten metre circles without incident.

'Looking good, team!' Norah cried. 'Let's thread the needle!'

Norah crossed the centre line first, then Sofia, closely followed by William. Aware they were lagging behind, Kristy sat deep in the saddle and urged Cassius on. He sprang forwards into a beautiful extended trot and crossed the centre line whiskers from Copper's tail. Kristy felt as if she was floating on air.

'Not bad at all!' called Norah. 'Pair up at A and then ride down to C for the salute.'

Kristy was so busy congratulating herself on a half-decent performance that she didn't realise she had covered far more ground than Copper. When she turned up the centre line the chestnut gelding was still a few strides behind.

'Hey, wait up! William shouted crossly.

Cassius plunged forward as if he had been stung by a bee, pulling the reins straight through Kristy's fingers. He whirled around, as fast as a spinning top, throwing her out of the saddle. Feeling her balance slipping, she grabbed hold of his mane and clamped her legs to his sides. The Percheron flung his head up, bashing her in the face.

Kristy's head snapped back and she clutched her nose in agony, fighting waves of dizziness that threatened to topple her from the saddle as efficiently as a chainsaw felling a fir tree. Her eyes were streaming and she touched her face gingerly. It felt warm and sticky. She checked her glove. It was covered in blood.

Cassius had finally stopped plunging but was trembling violently as he looked around, his nostrils flared. Kristy threw her arms around his neck, not caring that her nose was still throbbing painfully.

'It's alright, Cassius, you're safe with me,' she crooned. 'It was only William and Copper, coming up on your blind side.'

Gradually Cassius stopped trembling but Kristy kept stroking his neck and talking to him softly until she was sure he was calm.

'What on earth was all that about?' said William.

Norah was approaching, her face like thunder, and Kristy sighed inwardly. No doubt she was about to get a dressing down for not being able to control her horse. But to her surprise, Norah's anger was aimed firmly at her brother.

'What were you playing at, yelling on Cassius's blind side?' she hissed furiously. 'Do you ever engage your brain before you open your big mouth? He could have thrown Kristy off. As it is, she's probably broken her nose and won't be able to ride in the quadrille.'

Kristy touched her nose automatically. It felt tender, but

that was all. 'I don't think it's broken,' she said thickly. To her embarrassment her voice sounded feeble and quavery.

'Are you alright?' said Norah, looking hard at her.

Kristy nodded. 'I might just walk Cassius around the school for a bit to make sure he's settled.'

'Come and find us in the tack room when you're finished. And take this,' she said, handing Kristy a blue handkerchief. 'Your face is a mess.'

Norah beckoned the others to follow her so Kristy had the indoor school to herself. She dabbed her nose with the handkerchief until it had stopped bleeding and walked Cassius around on a long rein until her heart rate had returned to normal and his breathing was slow and steady.

She looked down at her blood-splattered jacket and groaned. If her parents even had an inkling that Cassius had had a minor meltdown while she was riding they would ban her from Mill Farm Stables in a heartbeat. They wouldn't understand that the big Percheron didn't have a malicious bone in his body, and he'd only acted like that because he'd been frightened.

'Oh Cassius, what are we going to do with you?' she said, jumping off and holding his broad face in her hands. She gazed into his blind eye. Apart from the slight cloudiness, you'd never know it didn't work. Cassius dropped his head and rested it in her arms.

'I'd never put you in any danger, Cassius,' she whispered in his ear. 'You need to trust me.'

⁓

THEY WERE in the tack room, waiting for her. William took Cassius's saddle and bridle from Kristy. Sofia handed her a mug of hot chocolate. Norah patted the sofa beside her. Kristy sat down obediently.

'How's your nose?' Norah asked.

'Fine,' said Kristy. 'I'm sorry I messed up.'

William shook his head. 'It was my fault. Norah's right. For once.'

Norah sprang to her feet. 'You always have to have the last word, don't you? If you must know -'

Kristy felt her patience snap. It had been a long and emotional morning. 'For pity's sake, will you two *please* stop arguing?' she cried. 'It's driving me mad.'

'And me,' said Sofia. 'You should hear yourselves. You sound like stroppy toddlers. I've a good mind to pull out of the team.'

'You can't do that!' said Norah, horrified.

'I can and I will. This is supposed to be fun, remember. Listening to you two constantly bickering is NOT fun.'

The twins looked at each other sheepishly.

'No more arguing, we promise,' said William.

Norah nodded. 'The team comes first.'

'Thank goodness for that, eh Kristy?' Sofia exclaimed. 'Hey, are you OK?'

Kristy was sitting slumped on the sofa with her head in her hands. Norah sat back down and put her arm around her shoulder. 'What's the matter?'

Kristy lifted her head and looked at them blankly. 'Isn't it all immaterial? If Cassius is going to go to pieces every time he hears a noise on his blind side then we don't have a chance. End of story.'

14

THE THIRTEENTH HORSE

*N*orah gave Kristy a gentle shake. 'Don't be so defeatist. For every problem there is a solution. We just need to work out what it is.'

Kristy wished she shared Norah's can-do attitude, but she was clean out of ideas. 'He doesn't trust me, that's the problem,' she said sadly.

'Yes, he does,' said Sofia. 'Emma told me the other day that he goes much better for you than he did for his old owner. She said he's a different horse.'

'He's the thirteenth horse,' said Kristy quietly. 'Everyone knows that's unlucky. I'm not normally superstitious, but -'

Norah cut in. 'Now you're being ridiculous.'

They didn't notice the door swing open until Emma walked in, bringing a whoosh of cold air with her.

'Who's being ridiculous?' she said, heading for the kettle.

'Kristy,' said Sofia. 'Cassius had a meltdown during our practice. We need to find a way we can make sure it doesn't happen again.'

Emma made herself a coffee and perched on the arm of the sofa. 'Something must have happened to set him off.'

'I rode up on his blind side and accidentally frightened him,' said William.

'How was he otherwise?'

'Every other time someone passed us it was on his good side and he was absolutely fine.' Kristy pictured the Percheron's pricked ears and floaty extended trot. 'He was enjoying himself.'

Emma took a sip of her coffee. 'The way I see it you have two options. You redesign the routine so Cassius is never passed on his blind side. Or you try to desensitise him.'

'What does that mean?' asked Norah.

'Put literally, it means to make him less sensitive to whatever is frightening him. You expose him over and over to whatever is causing the problem until he is so used to it that he no longer gets spooked.'

'You mean I need to keep riding up on his blind side and shouting?' said William with raised eyebrows.

'I think you should all join Kristy and Cassius for their schooling sessions until Cassius is completely used to other horses passing him in all directions.'

'But Kristy rides at half past six in the morning!' said William.

Norah eyed him beadily. 'What's more important - your beauty sleep or the team?'

He sighed. 'The team. Is that the right answer?'

Kristy could feel a flutter of something in her ribcage. She realised it was a tiny flicker of hope. She leaned forward and said, 'You think it'll work?'

Emma drained her coffee, stood up and smiled. 'You won't know until you try, will you?'

~

WHEN KRISTY'S dad dropped her off at the stables at half past six the following morning the others were already grooming their ponies, bleary-eyed but cheerful.

'I brought Cassius up for you. He's in the spare stable at the end,' said Sofia.

Touched by her kindness, Kristy fetched Cassius's tack and made a beeline for the stable. The Percheron was watching the activity in the yard with interest as the children darted back and forth, carrying tack and riding hats.

Kristy rubbed his poll. 'They're doing all this for us, you know.' He flicked an ear back at the sound of her voice and then whickered as Norah led Silver over to the mounting block. He seemed to have a soft spot for the plump grey gelding. 'You love being part of the gang, don't you?' she said fondly. Norah swung into the saddle and then looked at Kristy and pointed at her watch. Kristy found she was smiling as she reached for his bridle. 'So do I,' she told him fervently. 'So do I.'

THEY WALKED around the school on the left rein, Cassius first, then Jazz and Copper with Silver bringing up the rear.

Kristy looked over her shoulder at the others. 'OK, so what do we do?'

Norah kicked Silver into a trot until they were level with Kristy and Cassius. 'You stick to a walk today and we'll take it in turns to trot past you in both directions. We'll start on this rein so Cassius can see us and if that goes well we'll change reins and do the same on his blind side.'

'I think it's important everyone keeps talking so he can hear where we are,' said Sofia.

'Good idea,' said Norah. 'Hopefully by the time we introduce the music he'll be totally used to us passing him.'

On the left rein Cassius didn't bat an eyelid when the

others overtook him and his stride was long and easy. They changed reins and Kristy automatically tightened her reins.

'You've tensed up,' said Norah, eyeing her critically.

Kristy realised Norah was right. Her back and arms were rigid. She made a conscious effort to relax them and sit easily in the saddle.

'That's better. We're going to trot up behind you and we'll keep talking the whole time so Cassius knows we're here. I'll go first.'

As he heard Norah's voice behind him Cassius's muscles tautened and he swung his quarters around so he could see Silver. Kristy braced herself in case he threw his head up again, but to her relief he just had a good look and when she clicked her tongue and asked him to walk on, he did.

He stopped and swung around when Sofia and William rode past, too. Kristy tried not to stiffen up. Instead she concentrated on tuning into his rhythm by keeping her spine soft and straight and moving her hips in time with his stride. All the while she talked to him, keeping her voice low and steady. Gradually he stopped swinging his quarters around. When Norah checked her watch and told them it was twenty past seven and time to stop he was stiffening but not flinching as the others passed.

'He's cured!' cried Sofia.

'Not quite,' said Kristy. Positive energy was zinging though her body like electricity and she felt optimistic and buoyant. 'But I think we're getting there.'

~

BY THE FOLLOWING Sunday Cassius was so totally unfazed by Silver, Copper and Jazz trotting past him from all different directions that Kristy couldn't believe he had ever flipped out.

'Of course, Percherons are famous for being placid and good-natured,' said Emma, who had taken a five-minute break from mucking out to come and watch the children as they worked in the school together.

'We're going to introduce music next week,' said Kristy as she trotted past. 'I hope he's alright with that.'

'He'll be fine,' said Sofia. 'You worry too much.'

After their training session Kristy showed them the cardboard carrots she'd made for their snowmen noses.

William was the first to try his on. 'How do I look?'

'It suits you,' giggled Norah. She and Kristy pulled their noses on and began striking silly poses.

Sofia cleared her throat. 'I heard someone at school talking about the quadrille the other day. A girl in my year who rides at Coldblow.'

The others fell silent.

'They're entering a team. Karen, the owner, has decided to train them herself. They practice on a Sunday afternoon. This girl, Elsa, was bragging about how good they were. They're going as characters from Harry Potter, apparently. Harry, Ron, Hermione and Dumbledore.'

'That's not very wintery,' sniffed Norah.

'She reckons first prize is as good as theirs.'

'That's crazy. They don't even know who else is entering,' scoffed Kristy.

William slid the carrot from his nose to the top of his head like a paper party hat. 'Did you say they train on Sunday afternoons?'

'Yeah, why?'

'Let's go and spy on them. Suss out the competition.' His eyes were glinting roguishly, like they always did when he was planning a prank.

'How are we going to talk our way in? None of us have ever been to Coldblow before,' said Norah.

'That's where you're wrong,' said Sofia. 'Kristy has. She used to ride there. You can take us, can't you Kristy?'

15

TOUGH COMPETITION

*K*risty stood at the end of the immaculate Coldblow drive, which was flanked by immaculate horses grazing in immaculate paddocks, and turned to face the others.

'What if I forget what to say?'

'We've been through it a million times,' said William patiently. 'Tell Karen we're looking to move our ponies to a new yard and you'd recommended Coldblow because it had such amazing facilities and such brilliant trainers. Everyone loves to be flattered.'

'But what if she asks which yard you keep them at the moment?'

'Tell her. If Karen and Emma hate each other as much as we think, she'll be glad to steal three of her sister's liveries,' said Norah.

'What if Elsa recognises Sofia?' said Kristy, stalling for time.

Sofia shrugged. 'It doesn't matter. She knows I ride.'

Kristy sighed and set off towards the yard, the others close behind. It had been months since she'd last been to

Coldblow and she looked around her, seeing everything through a stranger's eyes. It was as spotless as it had always been, not a wisp of hay or a curl of shavings out of place. Karen, Kristy remembered, was fanatical about tidiness, and would bawl her grooms out if they left so much as a bucket or a yard broom where it shouldn't be. She had once been so impressed at the magazine-perfect yard, but it now felt cold and clinical compared to Mill Farm, where it didn't matter if the stable doors needed painting and the concrete was crumbling, because the horses and ponies were cosseted and content.

Kristy stopped. She could just make out strains of the Harry Potter theme tune coming from the direction of Coldblow's massive indoor arena.

'This way,' she said.

Unlike the indoor school at Mill Farm, which was really just an agricultural building converted into a makeshift menage, the indoor school at Coldblow was purpose-built with a full-size dressage arena and a small spectators' gallery. Kristy opened the door to the gallery and the four children slipped inside.

A tall woman wearing a hard hat and breeches was watching four identical dark bay ponies canter around the school, their strides matching the beat of the music perfectly. The two boys and two girls sat still and poised, their faces set in concentration as the woman barked orders at them.

'That's Karen,' whispered Kristy.

William's eyes were wide. 'She's even bossier than Norah!'

The riders split off on different reins, still riding beautiful collected canters. To Kristy they looked world-class, but Karen continued to pick faults. Their reins were too long, their shoulders too stiff, their backs not straight enough.

Sofia nudged her. 'They're going to thread the needle.'

They watched slack-jawed as the Coldblow team

executed perfect flying changes as they crossed over at the diagonal, passing each other so closely that Kristy was convinced they were going to collide.

The music was drawing to a crescendo and the riders had filed in behind each other as they cantered up the central line. Suddenly they peeled off into faultless pirouettes on alternate reins, the ponies appearing to dance to the music. Kristy realised she was holding her breath. It was spectacular.

The Coldblow team stopped, gave mechanical bows to the non-existent judge and walked their ponies on loose reins around the school.

'Wow, wow and double wow,' said Sofia. 'That was something else!'

Norah shrugged. 'It was OK. We can do better.'

'We can't, though, can we?' said William despondently.

Kristy grimaced. Karen was marching towards them.

'Looks like we've been spotted,' she muttered. She stood up and pasted a smile to her face. 'Hello there!'

'And you are -?' Karen left the sentence dangling as she inspected them with narrowed eyes.

'Kristy Moore. I used to ride here but I haven't been for a while.' Kristy recited the spiel she'd rehearsed about the others looking to move their ponies.

Karen gave them a flinty-eyed smile. 'And where do you keep them at the moment?'

'Mill Farm Stables,' said Norah. 'It's all a bit scruffy and amateurish down there to be honest. We're looking for somewhere a bit more -' she looked around her approvingly, '- professional.'

'Mill Farm Stables?' Karen repeated, her face clearing. 'No wonder you want to move. I can tell you from experience that Emma Miller does not run a tight ship. She's too soft to make a good businesswoman. Always was.'

Norah was warming to her role and began listing Mill Farm's shortcomings a bit too enthusiastically for Kristy's liking. She also didn't like the way Karen's mouth curled contemptuously as she criticised her sister. What was wrong with being soft? Kristy loved the way Emma treated the Mill Farm horses like they were her own children. Looking after animals should be a vocation, not a job.

'Do you give lessons?' asked Sofia.

'Only to the most able riders,' sniffed Karen. 'I have three other trainers who teach the rest.'

'But you teach these four?' Sofia waved her arm at the riders still walking their matching bays around the arena.

Karen gave her a patronising smile. 'This is my quadrille team. We're perfecting their routine for the Mayor's New Year's Eve show.'

'I heard about that,' said William. 'Competition's going to be pretty fierce, by all accounts.'

Karen gave a tinkle of laughter as brittle as breaking glass. 'Oh, I don't think so. They might as well engrave Coldblow's name on the trophy now. No other team stands a chance.'

'SHE'S SO ARROGANT!' fumed Kristy as the four children trailed back down the drive. How dare she assume the trophy's as good as hers?'

'Because her team is amazing?' Sofia replied glumly. 'I mean, pirouettes and flying changes. How are we supposed to compete with that?'

'I wonder if I would have been picked for the Coldblow team if we kept the ponies here,' said Norah, half to herself.

The others turned to her in horror.

'Norah! How could you even think that?' cried Kristy.

'The team comes first, that's what you said!' said Sofia.

William tutted. 'Don't ever have another go at me for not taking the competition seriously, sis.'

Norah stopped and the others almost cannoned into her. 'You've got to admit it's all pretty impressive. And then there's us, with our mis-matched ponies, our white onesies and our cardboard carrots. We're going to look ridiculous.'

Kristy's eyes blazed dangerously. 'No, we're not! We just need to keep practising until we're perfect. We stand just as much of a chance as they do.'

'Kristy's right,' said William. 'Think about it. Most people watching the show aren't going to know much about horses. They probably won't even notice the Coldblow team's fancy dressage moves. They just want to be entertained.' He ran a hand through his dark blond hair. 'We need to do something that's going to catch everyone's attention. Something that'll make us really stand out. Something unforgettable.'

'Like what?' said Sofia.

William grinned at them all. 'Leave it with me.'

16

THE ULTIMATUM

*K*risty was curled up on the sofa reading a feature on heavy horses in one of her old pony magazines when her mum sat down beside her and said in a serious voice, 'We need to talk.'

Kristy's heart sank. She had a nasty feeling she knew what was coming. Her history teacher, Mr Peterson, had called her to one side at the end of their lesson the previous afternoon. A thin, bespectacled man with an unusually large Adam's apple which bobbed up and down as he talked, he had laced his long bony fingers together and told her she needed to make more of an effort.

'I get the impression that you're a bright girl, Kristy. But your last assignment felt rushed and was filled with careless errors. I expect better.'

To make matters worse, Mr Baker had told her off for daydreaming again. Just because she hadn't been able to tell him which page of the textbook they were on. OK, so she might have lost concentration for a moment, but she had a lot on her mind.

Her mum took the magazine from her lap and folded it neatly on the coffee table.

'Your form teacher rang to say that a couple of teachers had concerns about your work. She asked if there were any problems at home. I was mortified.'

Crow's feet fanned out from her mum's greeny-grey eyes and frown lines creased her forehead. Kristy realised that the last few months must have been tough on her, too. Dad losing his job, having to move away from all her friends, swapping her beloved family home for their cramped apartment on the other side of town. She looked weary and worried.

'Sorry Mum,' she said in a small voice. 'I've just been a bit tired, that's all.'

'I *knew* this job would be too much on top of your schoolwork. You spend more time at those stables than you do at home. I've been talking to your father -'

Kristy's heart sank even further.

'- and he's convinced me that you should keep working at Mill Farm. He seems to think it's good for you. But on two conditions.'

Kristy felt light-headed with relief. 'Anything.'

'One, that you only ride on three mornings before school and just an hour on Sundays. We need some family time. And two, that you take more care over your schoolwork. Because I will be phoning your form teacher next week and if there is still even the slightest concern that your grades are slipping I will be banning you from the stables, OK?'

'OK,' said Kristy, nodding furiously.

He mum patted her knee and gave a wan smile. 'I know you think I'm being strict for the sake of it, but it's for your own good, Kristy. School is important. You have the rest of your life to spend with horses.'

~

KRISTY DECIDED NOT to tell the others about her mum's ultimatum. There was no point. They were already helping as much as they could. As long as her schoolwork improved everything would be fine. And if that meant no television until her grades picked up then it was a small price to pay. So, while her parents watched a film that evening she took herself off to her bedroom, re-wrote her history assignment and revised for a maths test the next day. By nine o'clock she was cross-eyed with tiredness and fell asleep as soon as her head touched the pillow.

On their way to Mill Farm the following morning Kristy thanked her dad for fighting her corner.

'That's OK, sweetheart. I know how much this job means to you. How are the rehearsals going?'

'Cassius doesn't mind the others passing him now, which is great, but I'm worried he might freak out when we try riding to music. William's bringing along his CD player this morning so I'll find out soon enough,' she sighed.

'Percherons are pretty unflappable, as I remember. I'm sure Cassius will be fine.'

As Kristy tacked the black gelding up she wished she could share her dad's confidence. The others had gone out of their way to help when Cassius had had his meltdown. They might not be so understanding if Kristy held them back again.

As it was, she needn't have worried. Cassius didn't bat an eyelid when William turned on the CD player and the rich sound of classical music filled the indoor school. Jazz, on the other hand, was a nervous wreck. She skittered around the school, bumping into the others and throwing her head around, her eyes rolling dramatically. Her honey-coloured flanks were dark with sweat and she stared, boggle-eyed, at

William's CD player as if it was a scary monster that was about to eat her alive.

'Steady Jazz,' murmured Sofia, running her hand along the mare's damp neck. But Jazz's flight instinct had taken over. Her tail was tucked into her hindquarters as she crabbed sideways across the school, spooked at Copper and tucked her head between her front legs.

'Be careful, she's going to buck!' cried Kristy, instinctively pushing Cassius towards the panicking mare.

She and the twins watched in horror as Jazz body twisted into three enormous corkscrew bucks. Miraculously, Sofia managed to stay on. But the whites of Jazz's eyes were still showing and Kristy could tell she wasn't finished yet.

'Turn the music off!' Kristy yelled to William. He jumped off Copper and sprinted over to the CD player. Silence restored, Jazz planted all four feet on the ground and stood shuddering, her ears flicking back and forth as she tried to work out if she was still in danger.

Cassius extended his neck and blew softly into the mare's nose, as if he was reassuring her that she was safe, and gradually she stopped shaking.

The four children looked at each other in silence. Sofia was the first to speak.

'I'm so sorry. I had no idea she would react like that.'

'It's OK. It could have happened to any of them,' said Kristy.

'Just when we'd sorted Cassius,' Norah sighed. 'I'm beginning to think we're destined to fail.'

'Don't be ridiculous,' said her brother.

Norah scowled. 'I don't remember any of the Coldblow team freaking out to the music while they were executing their perfect pirouettes, do you?'

Kristy thought hard. 'We need to desensitise Jazz to the

music, like we desensitised Cassius to being passed by other horses.'

'How are we going to do that?' said Sofia.

'Easy.' Kristy turned to William. 'Can Sofia borrow your CD player?'

'Sure.'

'Jazz's stable is next to the tack room, right? We need to leave the CD player on all night, playing on a loop. Quietly at first but getting louder and louder as she gets used to the music. I don't think she was playing Sofia up. She was genuinely frightened. Once she knows the music's not going to hurt her she'll be fine, I'm sure of it.'

Sofia shot Kristy a grateful look.

Kristy grinned back. 'Looking on the bright side, we now know that Jazz has natural rhythm.'

'What do you mean?' asked Norah.

'Didn't you notice,' Kristy giggled. 'Her bucks were perfectly in time with the music.'

THAT EVENING Kristy set the CD player up in the tack room. She found herself humming along to the music as she mucked out and filled haynets and water buckets. Although the day had started badly, things had improved. After her extra revision the night before she'd only dropped two marks in her maths test. And Mr Peterson had nodded approvingly when she'd found him in his classroom after lunch and handed him her re-written assignment. She couldn't wait to tell her mum.

When she led Jazz in from the field the palomino mare stopped in the doorway of her stable and listened, snorting softly. But Kristy was ready, clicking her tongue encouragingly and waving a bucket under her nose. Jazz gave her head a shake and followed Kristy in. Soon she was munching her supper happily. With any luck she would learn to associate music with food and wouldn't flip out again.

Kristy walked down to see Cassius with a swing in her step. He whinnied when he saw her.

'Is it me or the bucket you're so pleased to see?' she teased.

When he had finished wolfing down his supper he wandered over and nibbled her pockets, hoping for an extra treat. She found a mint and he crunched it noisily before resting his head on her shoulder and blowing warm, minty breath into her ear.

Kristy gave a sigh of contentment and wrapped her arms around his neck.

'Hey Cassius, do you know what?' she murmured. 'I really think our run of bad luck has come to an end.'

In the days that followed she wished that she could have taken back those words. Maybe if she hadn't tempted fate everything would have been alright. Common sense told her not to be so fanciful. But when she was alone, mulling over what happened, the fear that it was somehow all her fault settled like a cold, hard stone in the pit of her stomach and refused to go away.

17

FRIDAY THE THIRTEENTH

*I*t was Friday the thirteenth of December. An unlucky day, if you believed superstition. Kristy woke early, even though she wasn't riding before school, and peered out of the window. It was raining heavily. Fat raindrops chased each other down the glass, and in the street below their apartment rivulets of water disappeared into the gutters as fast as a raging waterfall.

Kristy thought of Cassius standing alone in his muddy field, his thick winter coat wringing wet, and she shivered. Percherons were bred to be hardy, but this rain was torrential. Emma would probably leave the others in until it stopped. There was one spare stable. Surely Cassius could use it, just this once? Kristy chewed a fingernail. If she was quick she had time to race over to Mill Farm and bring Cassius in. She pulled on her jeans and warmest jumper and crept down the hallway to the kitchen. As she passed her parents' room she could hear her dad snoring softly. She scribbled them a note, grabbed her waterproof coat and a woolly hat and slipped out of the front door.

By the time she arrived at the yard her eyelashes glistened

with raindrops and her jeans were soaked through. She found Emma in the barn hefting a bale of straw onto a wheelbarrow.

'I didn't think you were riding this morning?'

'I'm not. I was worried about Cassius. I wondered if he could go in the empty stable, just for today?' Kristy said breathlessly.

'I was going to bring him in anyway.' Emma waved her hand at the straw. 'I was just getting the stable ready.'

Kristy took the handles of the wheelbarrow. 'I'll do it. You sort out the others.'

Emma frowned at the pewter-coloured sky. Rain bounced off the yard and pooled in dips in the old concrete. 'I'm going to leave them all in until it clears. They'll probably go stir crazy but it can't be helped. Filthy weather,' she muttered.

Kristy pulled her hood over her hat, tucked her chin into her chest and pushed the wheelbarrow out of the barn. Horses and ponies watched over their stable doors as she negotiated the puddles. She could just make out the strains of their quadrille music over the sound of the rain and glanced over at Jazz, who looked as serene as a summer's day. They'd ridden to the music the previous morning and to their delight the mare hadn't flinched. Their plan seemed to be working, although Emma grumbled that she'd been put off classical music for life.

Kristy shook out the straw and filled a haynet and water bucket. She fetched Cassius's headcollar and ran down to his field. He was tucked up against the hedge, sheltering from the worst of the rain. Kristy splashed through the mud and felt his coat. It was sodden but he felt warm underneath.

Once he was in the stable she found an old towel in the tack room and dried him off as best she could. Emma appeared with his breakfast and handed it to Kristy, who set it down in front of him.

'I've got to take one of the liveries to a new yard this afternoon so I won't be back until at least five. Will you be OK getting them all in?' Emma said.

'Of course,' said Kristy. She'd brought all twelve horses in on her own a couple of times before and, although it was time-consuming, the horses were always ready to come in for their supper so she'd had no problem catching them.

'Thanks. I'll muck out the ponies so you don't have to do them, too.'

Kristy checked her watch. It was a quarter past seven. 'I'd better go.' She kissed Cassius and gave Emma a grateful smile. 'Thank you. I hated the thought of him out in this weather.'

'No problem. I'm not going to be able to sell my star quadrille horse if he's caught a chill, am I?'

Kristy felt like she'd been punched in the stomach. She shook her head, not trusting herself to speak, before turning on her heels and fleeing. She ran across the yard and down the long gravelled driveway, tears mingling with rain on her pale cheeks. As she hurried home she tried to pull herself together. Emma had always made it clear that she was planning to sell Cassius, and Kristy knew that that their time together was finite, yet it had been easy to ignore the truth. Over the last few weeks Kristy's every waking hour had been dominated by the quadrille. When she was with Sofia, Norah and William it was easy to fool herself into thinking she was just another owner who stabled her horse at Mill Farm. They were part of the gang. It was easy to pretend Cassius was hers.

She reached the steps to their apartment and ran an impatient hand across her face. She had to face facts. She was the hired help and no matter how many hours she slogged away mucking out other people's ponies she would never be able to afford her own. And it sucked.

∾

A STRONG WESTERLY wind had blown away the rainclouds by the time Kristy trudged back up to the stables after school. The yard was empty, which was no surprise. Most of the owners were fair weather riders, and they tended to stay away when it was cold and wet. Even Sofia and the twins had decided to stay at home.

Emma had been as good as her word and had mucked out all thirteen stables. Kristy mixed the feeds, following the list tacked onto the wall in the small and dusty feed room. Silver whinnied at the sound of the clattering buckets, which seemed to set off the others, so by the time Kristy came out they were careering around their fields, their hooves cutting into the mud like scythes through grass, their manes and tails rippling in the wind.

Kristy decided to get the horses in first and grabbed Viking's leather headcollar. The big bay warmblood shared a paddock with Jigsaw, Emma's handsome skewbald gelding. The two horses were charging up and down the post and rail fence as if their lives depended on it. As Kristy opened the gate Viking spooked at her and lost his footing in the mire. His legs started to buckle under him and for one terrible moment Kristy thought he was going to come crashing down.

'Steady!' she called. His legs scrambled wildly as he fought to regain his balance. To her relief he managed to stay on his feet. Jigsaw slid to a halt next to him, blowing hard. Kristy held Viking's headcollar behind her and took a couple of steps towards them. They last thing she wanted was for them to take off again.

She reached out a hand and the bay gelding sniffed it cautiously. She slipped the lead rope over his neck and slid his headcollar on before he had even noticed.

'Silly boy. You could have really hurt yourself.' She stroked his neck and looked at him sternly. 'Emma said you'd all go stir crazy and she was right. Have the lot of you been charging about pretending to be wild mustangs all afternoon?'

Viking followed her meekly out of the field and into his stable. She ran her hands down his legs but could feel no heat. 'Thank goodness for that. No harm done.' Kristy sighed with relief. 'Now for the others.'

One by one she led the horses in, picked out their feet and changed their rugs. Silver whinnied impatiently every time she passed his field, so she brought him in next, then Jazz, until just Copper and Cassius were left.

She slung Copper's navy blue headcollar over her shoulder and marched over to his field. The chestnut gelding was standing with his back to her in the far corner. She called him. Usually he would wander over but today he stayed where he was. Kristy sighed. Bringing the horses in was taking way longer than she'd thought it would.

When she drew nearer and Copper still didn't come over Kristy felt a prickle of foreboding. 'Come on, Copper, it's time for supper,' she called. The chestnut gelding turned to watch her but still didn't move. Kristy knew something must be wrong. Colic? she thought wildly. But horses with colic pawed the ground and kicked their stomachs, didn't they? Then she realised with horror that the bottom of his wide blaze was tinged with pink.

And his near foreleg was caught in the wire fence.

18

TRAPPED

*K*risty spoke softly as she approached the chestnut gelding. He pulled at the fence and squealed in pain as the wire tightened around his fetlock.

'Oh Copper, what have you done?' Kristy murmured, assessing the damage. His white sock was stained red and Kristy could see a flap of skin hanging loose just below his fetlock. It would need washing out and dressing. But her priority was to free him from the fence. Otherwise every time he pulled he would cause more damage. She ran a hand down his damp neck as she worked out what to do. Copper must have pawed the fence and somehow his hoof had slipped through one of the squares in the stock wire attached to the post and rail fencing. As he had panicked and tried to pull away it had closed like a vice, cutting into his skin.

Talking to him softly, Kristy ran her hand down his leg. She worked at the wire with her fingers, untwisting and loosening it. When a crow flew right over their heads, cawing loudly, Copper flinched and pulled back, undoing all Kristy's work. She started again, concentrating on de-tangling the wire, trying hard not to look at his poor broken skin because every time she did she felt a wave of queasiness rise in her stomach.

'It's OK,' she whispered. 'You'll be OK. I just need to -' Copper shifted his weight and the wire tightened again, this time trapping Kristy's fingers against his fetlock. She gasped in pain and sank to her knees. A sob rose at the back of her throat. It was no good. They were both trapped like rabbits in a snare. They'd have to stay where they were, enmeshed in the wire fencing, until Emma arrived home. Kristy craned her neck to look at her watch. It was half past five. Emma might not be home for an hour at least.

The sob escaped and Kristy's eyes filled with tears. 'Oh Copper, what can I do?' she wailed.

At the sound of her voice the chestnut gelding lowered his head and blew into her hair. It had an instant effect, snapping her out of her misery. He had been in agony for goodness only knew how long, yet he was being so brave. And here she was, giving up and crying like a baby.

Pull yourself together, Kristy, she told herself sternly. *You can do it.* Using her left hand, she concentrated on one small section of the wire, tugging and twisting, flexing and bending it until her fingers were sore and her breath was coming out in gasps. She could sense the wire weakening and upped her efforts.

After what seemed like an age the wire broke in two. Kristy felt blood rush back into her fingers. She eased Copper's foot out of the fence and set it gently on the muddy ground.

Standing up stiffly, she led the gelding slowly across the field, swivelling her head back every couple of paces to check he was OK. Miraculously, he didn't seem to be lame, although Kristy knew it was crucial she cleaned out the wound so it didn't become infected.

Once they were back in the yard she tied Copper up

outside his stable, gave him a haynet and began hosing down his leg.

He shook his head as the cold water trickled over his fetlock.

'It's freezing, I know, but I need to make sure there's no mud in your cuts,' Kristy told him.

When the water was running clear and Kristy was satisfied she had cleaned the wound thoroughly she turned off the hose and bent down to examine the wound.

What to do now? she wondered. Should she bandage it or leave it open? She remembered the first aid kit for horses Emma kept in the tack room and sprinted across the yard to fetch it. Inside were poultices and cotton wool, dressings and packs of saline solution, a thermometer and various antiseptic gels, powders and sprays. She picked a wound powder, a non-stick dressing and a bandage and ran back to Copper.

She was carefully bandaging his fetlock when Emma pulled into the yard in her horse lorry.

The older woman's face turned pale as Kristy recounted what had happened and she ran a hand through her hair. 'Thank goodness you found him when you did!'

'I've washed it out as best I could. Will you check it's OK?'

Emma nodded. Kristy stroked Copper's nose while Emma knelt down, untied the bandage and inspected the cut.

'Good job, Kristy. It looks clean to me. I don't think the cut needs a stitch and there's no swelling there. I can't feel any heat, either, and he's up-to-date with his tetanus. We'll keep him in for a few days and keep an eye on it. But I'd say he's been pretty lucky. The cuts are superficial. And he's got you to thank. I dread to think how much damage he might have done if you hadn't freed his leg.'

Kristy waved off the thanks. 'Anyone would have done the same,' she said. And then a terrible thought struck her. 'Do you think he'll be OK for the quadrille?'

Emma rested a hand on Copper's withers and gazed into the middle distance. 'Honestly? I don't know.'

~

WILLIAM'S FACE was stricken as he climbed slowly out of his mum's car, Norah close behind him. His normally mischievous eyes were red and puffy and his hands were balled into fists at his sides.

Kristy touched his arm. 'He's going to be fine.'

William nodded mutely. 'I know. Emma said. Sorry Kristy, but I just need to see him.'

Kristy joined Norah and they watched him disappear into Copper's stable.

'He looks really upset,' said Kristy, surprised.

Norah gave a little shake of her head. 'Copper means the world to him. I know you'd never guess, but he's as soft as marshmallow under that jokey exterior.'

Kristy took a deep breath. 'Emma said he might not be fit to ride in the quadrille.'

'I know.' Norah's voice was heavy. 'I told you we were doomed to fail.'

~

KRISTY SAT in the library and piled her books on the desk. She had a mountain of homework to do, but she couldn't tear her thoughts away from Copper and his poor leg. If only she'd noticed him standing by the fence not moving, when all the others were galloping around like lunatics. Emma was treating her like some kind of hero, yet she might have been able to stop Copper getting his leg stuck in the first place if she'd decided to get the ponies in first.

She was half-heartedly flicking through her English textbook when Sofia sat down next to her, followed closely by Norah and William.

'We need to have an emergency meeting,' Norah whispered out of the corner of her mouth. 'To talk about what we're going to do if Copper isn't better in time.'

Kristy fiddled with the zip on her rucksack. An idea had occurred to her the previous evening. She had examined it from all angles and although it grieved her heart to say so, she knew it made perfect sense.

'William should ride Cassius,' she blurted, avoiding an annoyed glance from a studious-looking boy sitting one desk along.

'*What?*' Sofia exploded.

'It's the only solution,' Kristy said. 'I drop out, William rides Cassius and you ride as a team of three.'

Kristy could see Norah's mind whirring furiously. 'That could work. The routine wouldn't be as symmetrical but that doesn't matter if we -'

'No,' said William firmly.

The studious-looking boy shot them a filthy look, gathered his books and stalked off to a desk at the far side of the library.

'Why not?' said Norah incredulously. 'After all, we only asked her in the first place to make up the numbers.'

'*Norah!*' said Sofia, her eyes wide.

Kristy gave them all a wan smile. 'She's right, though, isn't she?'

William rounded on his sister. 'Kristy is as much a part of the team as I am. As you are. Why should she give up her place for me? If it hadn't been for her, Copper might have damaged his leg so badly I might never have ridden again.'

'I agree,' said Sofia, staring Norah down. 'If Kristy doesn't ride, neither do I.'

Norah was silent.

'And think about it. Quadrilles are for four people, that's the whole point of them. If we only field a team of three we'd probably get eliminated anyway.' William nudged his sister in the ribs. 'So Kristy stays, OK?'

Norah lifted her shoulders in an exaggerated shrug. 'Alright, Kristy stays. But I don't know what we'll do if Copper isn't sound in time.'

'We'll assume he'll be alright and we'll carry on practicing,' said Sofia. She looked around at their worried faces. 'He'll be OK, I'm convinced of it.'

Kristy wasn't a natural pessimist, but she had seen Copper's torn fetlock and she found it hard to share Sofia's optimism.

SISTERS AND RIVALS

*W*illiam was back on his favourite yard broom for their training session on Saturday afternoon. He had found another piece of music by the same composer for them to ride to.

Norah gathered them in the middle of the school and asked them in turn what they were working on.

'I'm still getting Jazz used to riding to music. She's so much better than she was, but I want her to get to the stage where she doesn't even notice it's playing,' said Sofia.

'I want to practice my twenty metre circles and serpentines, making them as even as possible,' said Kristy. Like many horses, Cassius favoured his left rein and sometimes tried to swing his quarters out on his right rein, losing the shape of his circle. When she'd asked Emma for advice on how to fix the problem, Emma had told her to keep her inside leg on the girth to keep up momentum, and her outside leg back to stop him swinging his quarters out. She was keen to put it into practice.

Norah said she wanted to run through the ten metre circles from the centre line.

'What about you, William?' she asked.

William patted the handle of the broom and smirked. 'I don't really need to practice anything. My mount is pretty well perfect. I'll just run through the routine with him.'

Norah harrumphed. 'Perfect indeed! Well, make sure you don't get under our feet.'

They were so engrossed in their own drills that they didn't notice the door to the school open and a figure slip in. Kristy was completing what she hoped was a passable serpentine when she trotted past and pulled Cassius up sharply.

'Karen!' she squeaked. 'What are you doing here?'

Even though Kristy had a considerable height advantage, Karen still managed to look down her nose at her.

'I gather Mill Farm is entering a team for the quadrille. I'm presuming you're it?'

Sofia and Norah rode alongside Kristy and William ambled over, trailing his broom behind him. Kristy, trapped by the full force of Karen's glare, gave a small nod.

'I did wonder why you turned up last weekend. I didn't think your story rang true. So, when I heard on the grapevine my sister was entering a team, I thought I'd pop over and see what we were up against,' said Karen. Her lips curled disdainfully. 'Not much by the look of it.'

The smile on Norah's face froze.

'Where is she, anyway?'

'Right here,' said Emma, stepping out of the shadows. 'It's lovely to see you, Karen, as always,' she said, her voice heavy with sarcasm.

Kristy found her head swivelling from one sister to the other as if she was watching a tennis match. Now they were standing next to each other it was obvious the two women were closely related. Both were tall and slim-built, with blonde hair and porcelain-blue eyes. But that was where the likeness ended. Emma's eyes sparkled like the Mediterranean. Karen's were as cold and flat as the North Sea. While the lines etched on Emma's face were laughter lines, fanning out from her eyes like the prongs of a rake, Karen's were deep grooves between her eyebrows caused by constant frowning.

Now Karen knew the twins and Sofia had no intention of moving their ponies to Coldblow, all pretence of civility had vanished.

'I wish I could say the same, sister dear,' she mocked.

'So, to what do we owe this pleasure?'

Karen smiled nastily. 'I was just telling your team that I came to have a look at the competition. But I don't think we have too much to fear from four clueless kids, two scruffy ponies, one carthorse and a broomstick. It's probably safe to say the £1,000 prize money is mine.'

Kristy's mouth dropped open and she could hear sharp intakes of breath from Sofia and William.

'I didn't know there was prize money,' said Norah.

'Believe me, I wouldn't bother with a tinpot competition like this otherwise,' Karen sneered. 'I'm going to treat myself to a new dressage saddle when I win.'

Emma took a step forward. 'I shouldn't get too carried away if I were you. You haven't actually won yet. And anyway, shouldn't the money be split between your team?'

'You always were so annoyingly *nice*,' Karen spat back. 'Why should I? It's my yard, my horses, my team. And my prize money.' She turned on her heels and stalked out of the school. As she disappeared through the doors she called over her shoulder, 'See you on New Year's Eve.'

The four children looked at each other in shock.

'Sorry about my sister. She's what you might call an *acquired taste,*' Emma grimaced.

'You're so different to her,' said Kristy, her eyes wide.

'She always had a chip on her shoulder about being the youngest in the family. I'm afraid it made her very competitive.'

'I can't believe she called us clueless,' fumed Sofia.

'She was so rude about my broom,' said William.

'She called Cassius a carthorse!' cried Kristy.

'But she's right about one thing,' said Norah gloomily. 'The money is as good as hers. There's no way we're going to beat her.'

Emma ruffled Cassius's forelock and smiled at them. 'It doesn't seem fair that the Coldblow riders have their own personal trainer and you don't. How do you feel about me taking on the job?'

Kristy could see conflicting emotions cross Norah's face.

'Would I still be in charge of the routine?' she asked.

'Of course,' said Emma. 'You could be director of operations and I'll manage training and development.'

Norah considered this. 'I suppose it could work. As long as I have the casting vote when it comes to decision-making.'

'Absolutely,' said Emma. 'You're the boss.'

William pointed the end of the broom handle at his sister. 'Actually, Sofia is the boss.'

'Why do you always have to be so annoying?' said Norah.

Emma held up her hands. 'No arguing, you two. United we stand, divided we fall.'

'Eh?' said the twins in unison.

'We need to work together as a team if we stand any chance of winning. So, whenever you feel like bickering, just remember how fantastic it would be to wipe that smug expression off my sister's face, OK? She may think she's got an advantage with her perfect show ponies and her fancy routine, but you have grit, determination and friendship on your side. And that could make all the difference.'

~

THAT EVENING, as Kristy sewed pom poms onto their costumes, she mulled over Karen's visit. Like the others, she'd had no idea the Mayor was offering £1,000 in prize money to the winning quadrille team. Imagine if, against all odds, they did win and split the money between them. She'd have £250! It seemed like an enormous sum of money. But even if she added it to her wages from Mill Farm and the seventeen pounds, twenty-three pence and shiny silver button in her savings, it was no way near the amount Emma would want for Cassius. Would Emma take the money as a down payment, on the condition that Kristy paid the rest out of her wages? Kristy knew in her heart it was never going to happen. It would take her years to pay that kind of money back, and although Emma loved her horses like her own family, she was running a business, not a charity. And even if she did, Kristy could never in a million years afford the livery fees for the big Percheron.

The pom pom in her hand blurred as her eyes pricked with tears. She could dream all she liked, but in the real world Cassius would never be hers.

20

ACHILLES HEEL

*K*risty was sweeping the yard the next evening when William raced over.

'Have you nearly finished?' he said breathlessly. 'I've called a team meeting. There's something we need to discuss.'

'Just the ponies' rugs to change,' said Kristy, brushing her fringe out of her eyes. 'Why, what's happened now?'

William wrestled the broom from her clasp. 'You'll find out in a minute. Go and do the rugs. I'll finish this.'

As she changed Silver's rug Kristy wondered what new disaster had befallen them. Perhaps the vet had decided Copper wouldn't be sound in time and they were going to have to pull out of the competition. Perhaps - and her heart clenched painfully at the thought - Emma had found a buyer for Cassius. But no, she wouldn't do that before the quadrille, would she?

Kristy flew into the tack room. Norah and Sofia were either end of the sofa but William was nowhere to be seen.

'What's happened?' Kristy asked.

Norah folded her arms across her chest. 'I've no idea. William called this meeting, not me.'

'He's gone to get his phone. He said he's got something to show us,' said Sofia.

They could hear William whistling to himself as he crossed the yard and let himself into the tack room. 'Good, we're all here,' he said, tapping away at his mobile. 'I want you to watch this video.'

He set the phone down and pressed play. They watched six riders galloping their ponies up and down a line of poles, dropping balls
in buckets, placing flags in holders and leaping on and off with the ease of cowboys.

Norah tutted. 'We're riding a quadrille. Why are we watching mounted games?'

'Because I wanted you to see how they vaulted on. Look.' William zoomed in as a girl with a long, brown plait ran alongside a strawberry roan pony. She grabbed the reins and a hunk of mane with her left hand and held the front of the saddle with her right. Running alongside the pony's shoulder, she jumped forward with both legs and sprang up, throwing her right leg over the saddle and righting herself before galloping off.

'Impressive,' said Sofia.

'Exactly!' said William. 'I want us to lead the ponies in and vault on as part of our routine.'

'You want us to do *what?*' spluttered Norah.

'It's daring and it's different. The audience'll love it. We may not be able to do piaffes and flying changes, but we can do something extraordinary that'll wow the judges,' said William. 'What d'you think?'

'I think it's a brilliant idea,' said Sofia.

'You would say that. You used to compete in mounted games,' said Norah. She turned to Kristy. 'Tell them it's ridiculous and we're not doing it.'

Kristy had never vaulted on a pony in her life, but she had

loved gymnastics since she was tiny, and could vault on a gym horse with her eyes closed. Jumping on Cassius couldn't be so different, could it?

'Sorry, Norah. I'm with William and Sofia. We should have a go, at least. And then we can decide,' she said.

William beamed. 'The motion is carried.'

⁓

KRISTY STARED at her reflection in the mirror of the girls' toilets and sighed. Her hair was a mess but she'd left her brush at home. She was combing through it with her fingers, trying to pull out the worst of the tangles, when she became aware of a noise coming from one of the cubicles behind her.

She swung around and listened. Someone was crying. Without thinking, she sidled over to the cubicle and tapped gently on the door.

'Excuse me, are you alright?'

A small voice said, 'Not really.'

Kristy's eyebrows shot up. 'Norah, is that you?'

A nose was blown noisily and the bolt slid open. Norah's face was blotchy and her eyes were pink and puffy.

'Hey, what's happened?' said Kristy.

'Nothing. I'm fine. Well, I'm not ill or anything.'

Kristy fished in the pocket of her skirt and handed Norah a clean tissue. 'Want to talk about it?'

Norah's blonde curls bounced as she shook her head. 'There's no point.'

Kristy touched her arm. 'You never know, I might actually be able to help.'

Norah splashed water on her face and patted it dry with a paper towel. She looked at Kristy in the mirror. 'I can't vault,' she said tonelessly.

'Oh, I see.'

'William deliberately chose something he knows I can't do to humiliate me.'

'I don't think -' stammered Kristy.

'Silver's the smallest pony in the team but I can't even get on without a mounting block. I'm useless.' Norah gave a twisted smile. 'So now you know.'

'I'll teach you!' The words were out before Kristy had a chance to stop them.

'Why would you bother helping me?'

Kristy wasn't certain herself, if she was honest. Norah hadn't exactly welcomed her onto the team with open arms. And she could be so overbearing, ordering them all about as if they were a bunch of naughty toddlers. Did Kristy want to help out of the goodness of her heart, or did she want the chance to boss Norah about for a change? She wasn't one hundred per cent sure. But the fact was, if Norah couldn't vault, the team was in trouble. And the team came first.

'Does it matter why? I want to help, that's all that counts. Meet me in the gym at lunchtime. I'll have you vaulting like an expert in no time.'

~

KRISTY PATTED the worn leather top of the wooden gym vault horse and smiled at Norah.

'So, for the purposes of this afternoon's lesson, this gym horse is Silver. It's actually about the right height. You need to hold his reins - we'll use this piece of rope for today - in your left hand and hold the front of the saddle on the right-hand side with your right hand. You'll have to use your imagination for that. Keep in line with Silver's shoulders and, while you're looking straight ahead, bounce on both feet and propel yourself onto the saddle, swinging your right leg up and over your pony.'

Kristy bounced on the balls of her feet and sprang agilely onto the gym horse. She grinned at Norah. 'Just like that.'

'You make it look easy,' grumbled Norah.

'It is easy on the sprung floor,' said Kristy, jumping back down again. 'The bounce is the most important part to get right. If you do it properly it'll ping you into the saddle, I promise. Now you have a go.'

Norah glared at Kristy, clutched the pretend reins and bounced half-heartedly on the floor. She lurched onto the leather top but didn't have the momentum to swing her leg over and slid back down.

'I told you I can't vault.'

'Don't be so defeatist. Remember what you told me. "For every problem there is a solution. We just need to work out what it is."'

Norah scowled.

Kristy's eyes fell on a mini trampoline in the far corner of the gym. She placed it on the floor by the gym horse's shoulder. 'Bounce on that until the count of three and then vault on. I'll help you swing your leg over.'

Norah grabbed the reins again and bounced.

'One, two, THREE!' cried Kristy. She grabbed Norah under the armpits and pushed her into the air. Norah swung her right leg back, kicking Kristy in the mouth.

'Ow!' Kristy groaned, clutching her jaw.

'Sorry,' said Norah, beaming down at her from the top of the gym horse. 'At least your pain wasn't in vain. I did it! I vaulted on!'

'That's brilliant,' Kristy muttered. She rubbed her jaw and held out a hand. 'Let's see you do it on your own this time.'

Norah spent the next twenty minutes jumping on and off the gym horse. Once she could do it with ease Kristy took the mini trampoline away. After a couple of attempts Norah executed a perfect vault from the ground. She patted the leather top as if it was a real pony and then bowed to an imaginary audience.

'I am a vaulting queen!' she declared, sliding off the gym horse and high-fiving Kristy.

'Vaulting on a moving pony is going to be much harder,' Kristy pointed out, feeling a prickle of guilt as Norah's face fell. 'But if you can achieve that in just one hour you'll soon get the hang of it.'

Norah's confidence restored, the two girls collected their bags and headed for the corridor. As they prepared to go their separate ways Norah grabbed Kristy's hand.

'Thanks for helping me. I really appreciate it.'

'No worries,' said Kristy. Despite her earlier misgivings, she had enjoyed herself. 'It was fun.'

21

SMILE FOR THE CAMERA

*S*omething weird happened as Kristy led Cassius into the indoor school. He may have been unusually small for a Percheron, but he seemed to grow before her very eyes. He was as solid as a wall and just as tall. She'd told herself - and the others - that she'd be able to vault on him, no problem. But who was she kidding? He was a whole hand higher than Jazz and twice as broad. She led him over to where Norah was standing with Silver and tried to keep her nerves in check.

'Ready?' said Norah, who looked decidedly green.

Kristy's palms felt slippery with sweat and she wiped them on her jodhpurs. She nodded. 'As I'll ever be.'

'I thought I had it tough, vaulting onto Silver. But how on earth are you going to jump onto Cassius. He's *enormous!*' said Norah.

'It'll be fine,' said Kristy, with more confidence than she felt. 'You just need to get the bounce right, remember. You go first.'

Norah bounced a couple of times and scrambled into the saddle. She punched the air with glee. 'Now your turn.'

Kristy gazed at the pommel of Cassius's saddle. It was as high as her shoulder. She grabbed the reins and a large handful of mane. She jumped up but gravity pulled her back down before she could swing her leg over Cassius's rump. He looked at her with his good eye. He seemed perplexed, as if he couldn't understand why on earth she wasn't using the mounting block like a normal human being.

'You nearly had it,' called Norah.

Kristy nodded. After weeks of mucking out and hefting buckets of water and bales of hay she was stronger than she'd ever been. It was all about confidence. She closed her eyes and visualised herself effortlessly leaping onto Cassius's back, as graceful as a circus rider.

She flexed her arms and tried again. On the count of three she planted both feet firmly on the ground and pushed up with her legs. She hauled herself into the saddle and soon she was staring down at Cassius's familiar pricked ears, a wide grin on her face. Graceful it wasn't, but she'd done it.

A SILVER FOUR-WHEEL drive was parked in the yard when Kristy and Norah led Cassius and Silver out of the indoor school.

Norah's hand flew to her mouth. 'It must be the vet! Mum asked him to come and have a look at Copper.'

A tall man with a weathered face and a salt and pepper beard was deep in conversation with Emma outside Copper's stable. William led the gelding out and the vet squatted down to have a look at his injured fetlock.

'You've been hosing down his leg?'

'Twice a day,' Emma confirmed.

He ran his hand down Copper's leg. 'There's no heat and

no swelling. And the cuts look as though they are healing nicely. Let's trot him up to see if he's sound.'

William walked Copper to the far end of the yard and trotted him back. He looked OK to Kristy but the vet scratched his beard and said, 'Once more, please.'

Kristy crossed her fingers as William trotted Copper up a second time. The vet patted the chestnut gelding's neck.

'It's a quadrille you want to do?' he asked.

William bobbed his head. 'We've entered a team in the New Year's Eve show. There's no jumping involved. We just trot in circles and serpentines and stuff. D'you think he'll be alright?'

Four pairs of worried eyes watched the vet as he picked up his medicine bag and clicked it shut. He cleared his throat. Kristy realised she was holding her breath.

'I'm happy he's sound. I'd recommend you wait a few more weeks before you jump him, but I think he's absolutely fine to take part in a quadrille.'

Kristy and Norah whooped and high-fived each other and William danced a little jig of happiness and cried, 'New Year's Eve show, here we come!'

~

IT WAS as if their luck changed the day the vet came. Training sessions, under Emma's eagle eye, went like clockwork. Kristy and Norah perfected their vaults and Jazz trotted around the indoor school completely unaffected by the music. Their circles were precise and their serpentines impeccably executed. Even Emma, who was the ultimate perfectionist, couldn't pick fault with their crossovers. Cassius was as fit as the ponies and his muscles rippled under his thick, glossy coat as he trotted in time to the music. Their confidence was sky high.

A couple of days before Christmas, Emma called them into the tack room.

'You've all worked so hard you deserve a few days off so I'm cancelling all training sessions for a week. Go home and enjoy Christmas with your families. And that includes you, Kristy. My cousin is staying with me over the holiday and she'll help with the horses. I'll see you all the day before New Year's Eve for a full dress rehearsal so make sure you bring your costumes.'

'Can I still come and see Cassius?' Kristy said, thinking of the big bag of carrots she'd bought him for Christmas.

'Of course you can. But you're not to lift a finger. I want you to take a well-deserved break.'

KRISTY PACKED her costume and Cassius's white sheet into a carrier bag, jumped down the steps of their apartment two at a time and set off towards the stables at a jog. Her heart felt as light as a feather. She'd enjoyed spending time with her mum and dad over Christmas, but after a week away from Mill Farm she was itching to be back with the horses.

She had almost reached the drive when she heard the hiss of air brakes and the bus pulled up behind her. To her surprise Sofia jumped off, clutching a large jute shopping bag.

'How come you're on the bus?' said Kristy.

'Dad's away and Mum's car's in the garage. I was going to cycle over but I didn't think I'd be able to manage with this,' Sofia said, holding up the bag. The limp arm of a white onesie fluttered in the wind.

The two girls chattered about Christmas as they walked up the drive. Norah and William were already grooming their ponies and Kristy raced down to the bottom paddock, impatient to see Cassius. She'd brought over the carrots on Christmas morning but hadn't seen him since.

Back at the yard, she set to work combing the tangles from his mane and tail and brushing his coat until it shone.

'I don't know why you're being so fussy. No-one's going to tell if he's clean under his sheet,' said Norah.

'I know, but he loves being groomed and I love grooming him,' said Kristy.

Norah disappeared into the tack room with Sofia to change into their costumes and Kristy grabbed her carrier bag and followed them.

Sofia handed her a stick of white face paint and a compact mirror.

'Really?' she said.

'Absolutely,' said Sofia. 'Emma wanted a full dress rehearsal, remember.'

The girls giggled as they pulled on their onesies, tied their scarves and painted their faces chalk-white. Kristy helped the others fix their carrot noses and fit their cardboard top hats over their riding helmets.

Norah held Sofia's compact mirror at arm's length and peered into it, cackling like a witch as she struck silly poses. 'We look awesome. Great costumes, Kristy!'

Kristy was about to brush the compliment aside but she stopped herself. Norah was right - the costumes *were* awesome. 'We do look pretty good, don't we?' she grinned.

Outside, Emma was taking photos of William and Copper. 'We'll get a couple of team shots,' she called.

Soon they were lining up, Cassius and Jazz flanking Copper and Silver. As Emma snapped away, Kristy couldn't keep the grin off her face. They looked amazing. They had worked so hard perfecting their routine. They were going to take the New Year's Eve show by storm. Happiness fizzed inside her like bubbles in a glass of lemonade.

'I want a couple of photos of Kristy and Cassius on their own before our rehearsal,' said Emma, summoning Kristy closer.

'Smile,' she told Kristy, as if she wasn't already beaming from ear to ear. Emma took half a dozen photos of them both, nodding approvingly as she scrolled through them. 'Just the job.'

'Just the job for what?' Norah asked.

'The online advert for Cassius. I'm going to upload it tonight.'

Kristy felt winded, as though someone had punched her in the stomach. And all the tiny bubbles of happiness fizzled away, like lemonade gone flat, leaving her feeling utterly deflated. And completely alone.

22

A FRIEND IN NEED

The tears Kristy had managed to contain throughout their dress rehearsal began trickling out as she climbed the steps to their apartment, and by the time she pushed open the front door they were in full flood. Her parents took one look at her and rushed over.

'Whatever's wrong?' her mum said, putting her arm around Kristy's shoulder and leading her to the sofa. Kristy hugged her knees and let the tears fall.

'Kristy?' said her mum, rubbing her back. 'Tell us what's happened.'

But the sobs had plugged Kristy's throat and she was unable to speak.

'Did you fall off,' said her dad. His voice was scratchy with worry. 'It's my fault if you did. I should never have let you ride a blind horse.'

'A *what*?' cried her mum.

Kristy shook her head. Her parents mustn't blame Cassius. He'd done nothing wrong. She swallowed the sobs and squeaked, 'I didn't fall off.'

Kristy's dad wiped away her tears with his thumbs. 'So,

what did happen? Did you have a falling out with your friends?'

'Emma wanted to take our photo before the dress rehearsal. I thought it was because she was proud of us.' Kristy's bottom lip wobbled. 'It wasn't that at all. She just wanted a nice photo for the advert for Cassius. She's putting it online tonight.'

Kristy's mum handed her a glass of water.

'You knew it was going to happen eventually,' she said.

Kristy stared into the glass. 'I thought she might change her mind and keep him.'

'I know how you feel, sweetheart. I know what it's like to lose something you love.' Kristy's mum sounded wistful. Kristy knew she was remembering their big, detached house with a view of the hills. But that was just bricks and mortar. There was no comparison.

'What if his new owner doesn't look after him properly? No-one will ever love him as much as I do,' she wailed, fresh tears pouring down her face.

Her dad lifted her chin. 'You need to be brave, angel. If I've learnt anything it's that life is a series of setbacks and if you pick yourself up, dust yourself off and keep going you'll be stronger for it. You knew you were only borrowing Cassius and that the time would come when you had to give him back. Emma will make sure he goes to a lovely, caring home. He'll be fine. And once your heart mends - and it will, I promise - you'll treasure your memories of him for the rest of your life.'

Kristy took the handkerchief he gave her and blew her nose noisily. She knew he was trying to help. But the leaden feeling in her heart refused to budge, as solid and intractable as a granite boulder. He was right in some respects. Emma would vet any potential homes. And Cassius would probably be fine. But he was so very wrong about one thing. Kristy's heart would never mend.

~

KRISTY WAS PUSHING her dinner about on her plate when the doorbell rang.

'Who on earth's that at this time of night?' said her mum.

'I'll just look into my crystal ball,' joked her dad, pushing his chair back. He'd spent the evening trying to tease Kristy out of her black mood. It hadn't worked.

Kristy stabbed a potato with her fork and started chewing. It tasted like dried shavings. She took a slug of water and swallowed.

The front door clicked open and the sound of voices drifted along the hallway. For a nano-second Kristy allowed herself to fantasise that it was Emma, finally realising how upset she was and coming to give her Cassius. But just as quickly she chastised herself for being so stupid. Stuff like that never happened to girls like her.

'Kristy, there's someone here to see you,' said her dad.

'Sofia! What are you doing here?'

Sofia looked as red-eyed as Kristy had when she'd looked in the mirror earlier. But why would Sofia be so upset about Emma selling Cassius? It didn't make sense.

Sofia grimaced. 'I've lost my costume.'

Kristy laughed, despite herself. 'I thought William was the joker, not you.'

'No, I really have. I left it on the bus on the way home from the stables. Mum tried ringing the bus depot but it's closed. The answerphone message says it won't be open again until Monday.'

'And the quadrille is tomorrow,' said Kristy slowly.

Sofia's green eyes welled. 'I'm such an idiot. We can't compete with only three costumes. Norah'll go mad. And all the hours Emma's spent helping us when she's so busy. All wasted. Oh, Kristy, what am I going to do? I've ruined it for everyone.'

Kristy was silent.

'Please don't hate me,' said Sofia pitifully.

Kristy waved her hand, gesturing Sofia to be quiet. An idea was forming in the back of her mind. 'We might be able to fix it. I ordered five onesies by accident. I was going to send one back, but Mum said she'd give it to my cousin for her birthday. It was the same size as the ones I ordered for you and William. You can wear that.'

'But what about the pom poms and carrots? And I haven't got a top hat.'

'I should have enough black wool and cardboard left over. We can make new ones tonight.'

'Are you sure?'

Kristy was grateful to have another drama to take her mind off Cassius. 'Of course I'm sure.'

The worry lines vanished from Sofia's forehead. 'Mum's waiting outside. I'd better ask her to pick me up in a couple of hours,' she said. And she sped out of the flat.

'Ask her if she's got a spare white sheet,' Kristy called as she thundered down the hallway.

By the time Sofia reappeared a few minutes later Kristy had cleared the breakfast bar and found the spare wool and cardboard.

'The only thing you won't have is the scarf,' she said, handing Sofia a ball of black wool and two cardboard discs.

Sofia reached into her shoulder bag. 'Aha, that's where you're wrong. It's the one thing I have got. It was so cold I wore it home.' Her lips twitched. 'I really am hopeless, aren't I?'

'Absolutely hopeless,' Kristy agreed.

~

THEY WORKED SOLIDLY for the next hour and a half, making and sewing on the pom poms and cutting out and painting the carrot nose and fiddly top hat. Kristy made a couple of ties and showed Sofia how to sew them onto her white sheet once she was home.

'Were the face paints in the bag you left on the bus?'

'No, thank goodness. Norah's got them. It was just the costume.' Sofia held her onesie against her and curtsied. 'How does it look?'

Kristy eyed her critically. 'One of the pom poms is a bit wonky but I don't suppose anyone'll notice. Otherwise it looks great.'

Sofia's expression was serious. 'You saved my life tonight, Kristy. Thank you.'

'Don't exaggerate. You would have sorted something out.'

'I mean it,' said the older girl fervently. 'You are a true friend.'

Kristy didn't reply, but that night, as she lay in bed trying to drift off to sleep, Sofia's words provided a modicum of happiness to her otherwise heavy heart.

23

NEW YEAR'S EVE

*N*ew Year's Eve dawned, cold and crisp. A crystalline hoar frost had formed overnight and tiny ice crystals, as dazzling as quartz, coated the steel handrail on the steps to Kristy's apartment.

'We'll see you there,' called Kristy's mum from the top step.

Kristy waved goodbye and set off at a brisk walk towards the centre of town. She wanted to see where the arena had been set up so she could report back to the others when she met them at the stables.

The pavement felt crunchy underfoot and overhanging branches sparkled as if they had been dipped in caster sugar.

The town square was already busy, even though the show wasn't due to start for another hour. Families were gliding hand-in-hand around the ice rink that had been set up in front of the town hall, and reindeers chewed hay and dozed in temporary pens behind it. As Kristy skirted a stall selling hot chocolates topped with white and pink marshmallows, a lorry pulled up beside her and a couple began unloading a team of overexcited huskies.

'I don't suppose you know where the quadrille competition is being held?' Kristy asked a woman dressed as an ice queen, who was handing out flyers for the icicle ball.

'In the car park,' said the woman, pointing to the side of the town hall.

Kristy wandered over and gasped. A temporary dressage arena with a sand surface had been built, complete with white boards. Rows of plastic seats four deep lined the two long sides of the arena and at the far end a raised platform had been erected, on which stood three more seats. For the Mayor and his two fellow judges, Kristy presumed. It all looked incredibly professional and the butterflies in Kristy's ribcage started fluttering wildly.

She checked her watch. It was nine o'clock. The show was due to start with the reindeer parade at ten, and the quadrille competition was scheduled for eleven. The Coldblow team would probably be travelling over in Karen's top-of-the-range horse box. The Mill Farm team were going to hack over and change into their costumes once they arrived.

A man wearing a pinstripe suit and a bowler hat began setting out the arena markers. Kristy sidled over and coughed politely.

'Excuse me, but do you know how many teams are entering?'

'Ten at the last count,' he said, placing the letter B by her feet. 'Why, are you coming to watch?'

'I'm riding in it, actually,' said Kristy shyly.

The man looked impressed. 'Good for you. It's nice to see young people taking part in community events.' He consulted his clipboard and strode towards the small stage. 'I think the M goes just about here, don't you?'

Kristy nodded. 'Yes, that looks about right.'

'Do you have your own pony?'

Kristy felt the usual lurch deep in the pit of her stomach whenever she thought about Cassius being sold. But she'd given herself an extra stern talking to on the walk into town. No more feeling sorry for herself. She was lucky to have been able to ride Cassius at all. Most kids never had opportunities like that. And even once he'd been sold, she'd still have her horse fix, working at Mill Farm. No, from now on she refused to wallow in self-pity. She straightened her shoulders and smiled.

'No. I'm just borrowing someone else's. But I'm OK with that.'

The man nodded approvingly. 'I like your attitude. Good luck for later. I'll keep an eye out for you.'

~

NORAH WAS STANDING in the middle of the yard directing operations like a hyperactive sergeant major. While she barked out a litany of orders, William and Sofia scurried about, fetching grooming kits and haynets and gathering buckets and bandages.

Kristy jogged over. 'How's it going?'

William plonked two haynets on the concrete and rolled his eyes. 'Norah has gone into overdrive.' He shot his sister a dark look. 'But she needs to be careful. If she doesn't stop bossing us about Sofia and I are going on strike. And then she'll have to do everything herself.'

Keen to avert a row, Kristy picked up the haynets and said, 'I'm here now. Just tell me what needs doing and I'll do it. It'll only take twenty minutes to ride over. We've still got masses of time.'

Emma had decided to drive to the show so they loaded her Land Rover with haynets, buckets, two huge canisters of water and their costumes.

'Kristy, you haven't even started grooming Cassius yet!' Norah shrieked.

'I spent an hour grooming him after the dress rehearsal yesterday and kept him in last night. He should just need a quick brush today,' she said mildly.

Kristy found Cassius's grooming kit and let herself into his stable. He was asleep, his bottom lip drooping and his whiskers twitching. Kristy wondered if he was dreaming about her. Although he had straw in his mane and tail, she was relieved to see that his thick coat was still shiny.

'Hey, handsome,' she whispered.

The Percheron's eyes snapped open. He tilted his head to look at her and whickered. Kristy set to work on his tail, brushing it until it cascaded like a wavy waterfall. She combed his mane and gave his coat a quick flick with a body brush before picking out his feet and oiling his hooves.

Nora, William and Sofia poked their heads over his stable door.

'He looks great,' said Sofia.

'I still think we should have plaited them,' Norah sighed.

'We took a vote and you lost. Three against one,' William reminded her.

'I bet the Coldblow team have plaited their ponies. Manes *and* tails,' said Norah.

Kristy screwed the cap back on the hoof oil and handed it to Norah. 'Don't worry about the other teams. So what if they've got perfect plaits and amazing costumes? Who cares if they can execute flawless flying changes? We've worked so hard for this competition and I've enjoyed every minute. I want to go out today with my best friends and have fun, don't you?'

'Well said,' said Emma appearing behind the twins and Sofia. She jangled the Land Rover keys. 'I'll see you off and then I'll head over.'

The four children looked at each other and grinned.

'Well, I guess this is it,' said Sofia.

'I feel sick,' said Norah, clutching her stomach.

William patted her shoulder like a kindly uncle. 'You'll be fine.'

All of a sudden Kristy's nerves had morphed into excitement and she couldn't wait to jump on Cassius and show everyone just how amazing he was.

'Come on,' she said impatiently. 'Let's do this!'

~

NORAH TURNED a ghostly shade of white when she saw how many people had turned out for the Mayor's first New Year's Eve show.

'There are millions here!' she cried.

'Not *millions*, sis. Maybe a couple of thousand,' said William.

Norah tugged on Silver's reins, stopping the little grey gelding in his tracks. 'I don't think I can do it,' she whispered.

'Don't be silly. Of course you can. Anyway, you've got no choice. You're our leader. You need to lead us into battle.' William smiled encouragingly at her.

Kristy met Sofia's gaze and raised her eyebrows. She had no idea Norah would be the one to suffer from nerves. She was always so assertive, so certain of herself. But William seemed to know how to handle her.

She checked her watch. It was five to eleven. 'Emma says we're last on. Let's watch a couple of the other teams before we get changed.'

The others followed her to the arena, where families were already taking their seats. At eleven o'clock on the dot a man wearing a pinstripe suit, a bowler hat and a flamboyant gold chain of office walked over to the raised platform and fiddled with the microphone.

'It's the dressage marker man!' Kristy said in surprise.

'The who?' said William.

'I met him earlier. I didn't realise he was the Mayor.'

The audience fell silent as the Mayor started speaking. 'Welcome everyone, to our very first quadrille competition, although I very much hope it won't be our last.' He smiled at them all. 'When I first decided to hold a New Year's Eve show to celebrate the end of one year and the beginning of another, my fellow councillors couldn't understand why I wanted to include a quadrille. What on earth have horses and riders in fancy dress riding to music got to do with New Year's Eve, they asked me.

'But what they didn't know is that once, a very, very long time ago, I competed in a quadrille competition just like this one. It was one of the best times of my life. Hard work, but such fun!' His eyes took on a faraway look. 'Unlike my team-mates I didn't have my own pony so I had to borrow one from the local stables. And the experience was enough to give me a lifelong love of horses. So, when I was thinking of events for our show I knew we had to have a quadrille. It was, as you young people say, a no brainer.

'And so, it gives me great pleasure to introduce our first quadrille team in this inaugural competition. Please give a huge round of applause to the ladies from the Southfield Riding Club!'

Two black horses and two dappled greys walked sedately into the ring to the sound of a wedding march. The women riding the greys were dressed in black morning suits, top hats and stick-on moustaches and the women atop the black horses wore meringue-like wedding dresses.

'They look amazing,' breathed Sofia.

'They should have spent more time practising than they

did on their costumes,' said William sagely, as one of the black horses broke into an extended trot across the diagonal, forcing the others to canter to keep up. As they rode up the centre line in pairs one of the grey mares snaked her head and bared her teeth at the black gelding beside her. He skittered away, almost unseating his rider. The crowd roared with laughter.

'Looks like they might be heading for the divorce courts before too long,' William joked.

'They're not a very forgiving audience,' Norah fretted.

Kristy knew Norah was worrying about the vault. She reached over and touched her arm. 'You'll be alright. It's all in the bounce, remember.'

Norah gave her a brief smile. 'I know.'

Emma marched over, four white sheets under her arm. 'Come on, we'd better get you in these costumes.'

They followed her to the Land Rover and took it in turns to change inside. Norah said she couldn't paint their faces as her hands were shaking too much, so Sofia took over, while Kristy and William fitted the horses' sheets and fixed their white exercise bandages.

Cardboard carrots on their noses and their top hats over their riding helmets, they knotted their scarves and rechecked girths and stirrup leathers. As they led their horses over to the arena they heard the recognisable notes of the Harry Potter theme tune.

'Coldblow must be before us,' said Sofia.

Sure enough, Harry, Ron, Hermione and Dumbledore were trotting into the arena on their four identical dark bay ponies and the Mill Farm team, standing in the small collecting area, had an uninterrupted view of their routine.

Kristy was surprised to realise that the Coldblow riders weren't as perfect as she remembered. On several occasions, their over-rehearsed ponies anticipated the transitions before their riders had given them the aids, which messed up their crossover and almost resulted in a two-way collision.

'They don't look very cheerful,' said Norah, surprised.

'Would you, if you were about to be on the receiving end of a dressing down from Karen?' said Sofia. 'I almost feel sorry for them. Almost, but not quite.'

The music built up to its crescendo and one of the ponies peeled off into a pirouette seconds before the others. His rider, a stocky boy with a face like thunder, gave the pony a sharp rap with his crop. Several people in the audience gasped and one man called out, 'Hey, that's not very sporting!'

The applause was muted as the Coldblow riders gave their mechanical bows to the Mayor and trotted out of the ring, staring straight ahead with granite faces as they passed the Mill Farm team.

Sofia, William and Kristy lined up behind Norah. Emma ruffled Silver's forelock and regarded her team. 'Unlike my sister, I don't care if you're first or last. I just want you to enjoy yourselves. You deserve to, after all your hard work. I'm super proud of you all. So, go out there and have fun. If you enjoy it, the audience will too. Good luck!'

The deep, rich sound of a cello cut through the air. It was their cue to go.

'Good luck everyone!' shouted Kristy, her eyes shining with excitement as she bounced on the balls of her feet. 'Let's smash it!'

～

NORAH RAN INTO THE ARENA, Silver trotting by her side. Kristy could see the tension in her friend's shoulders and she willed Norah to relax and enjoy herself. To believe in herself.

'You can do it!' she whispered. Norah grabbed a handful

of mane, matching Silver stride for stride. *Bounce, bounce, boing!* Kristy breathed a sigh of relief as Norah heaved herself into the saddle and trotted towards the judges. The crowd broke into applause.

One down, three to go.

With an effortless leap, Sofia was in the saddle. William shot a look over his shoulder.

'Good luck,' he mouthed, holding up crossed fingers.

Kristy gave him the thumbs up and laced her fingers through Cassius's mane to stop them trembling. Adrenalin was whizzing through her nervous system like a bullet through the barrel of a gun. She knew it was her fight or flight reflex and that she had to channel her nerves or the wobble in her fingers would travel down through her legs and all would be lost.

She focused on William as he flung his right leg over Copper's saddle with the casual ease of a cowboy.

'Our turn,' said Kristy. Once again Cassius seemed to be getting taller by the minute. Kristy clicked her tongue and he broke into a trot. *It's all in the bounce, all in the bounce.* The words echoed around her head as she ran alongside the Percheron.

She took a deep breath and imagined she was a rubber ball, her legs as bouncy as elastic. *One, two...three!* And suddenly she was kicking her legs up and sailing into the air, as light as a snowflake.

Time stood still as she reached the highest point, suspended in mid-air over Cassius's withers. But instead of landing in the saddle as she had done so many times before, her superhuman bounce propelled her right over the gelding's back and she landed with a stumble on his far side.

Someone in the audience shrieked with laughter and Kristy's cheeks burned under the layers of white face paint. It was her worst nightmare come true. All she needed now was for Cassius to turn into a broom.

Mortified, she glanced at the others, still trotting towards the Mayor, blissfully unaware of the catastrophe unfolding behind them. Would they notice if she slunk out of the arena and left them to it? Norah had been right all along. She was the weak link in the team. They were better off without her.

Cassius had slowed to a halt and Kristy gazed into his cloudy right eye, wondering what to do.

In a second, she made up her mind. She was being pathetic. Cassius was so brave. If she ran away now she'd be letting him down. Letting the team down. She turned towards the Mayor and gave him a rueful smile.

'I think I might try that again,' she said loudly.

The audience cheered and a woman whooped and shouted, 'You go, girl!'

Kristy darted back to Cassius's nearside and once again grabbed a handful of his mane. This time, as she planted both feet on the ground, her timing was perfect. And, as she vaulted into the saddle as gracefully as an Olympic gymnast, the crowd went wild.

24

A NEW OWNER

*A*fterwards, if anyone asked her how their quadrille went, Kristy could only reply, 'It began with a nightmare and ended like a dream'. For it was true. Once she'd caught up with William and Copper she forgot her disastrous start and began to enjoy herself. All the hours of rehearsals paid off, and from their first serpentine to the moment they cantered out again, their faces flushed with pleasure, it was just brilliant. Better than she could have imagined in any daydream, in fact. And Kristy loved to daydream.

That is not to say the rest of the routine was perfect. Cassius swung his quarters in a couple of times on his right rein, making their circles a bit egg-shaped, and Jazz rolled her eyes and shied dramatically at a toddler's pink cloud of candyfloss, much to the amusement of the people sitting nearby. Norah forgot to change her diagonal a couple of times in all the excitement and William's top hat fell off as they threaded the needle. But it was so obvious to everyone watching that the four children, the three ponies and the noble black Percheron were having the time of their lives, that their mistakes were forgiven and forgotten. And when they stood in a row and saluted the Mayor the crowd gave them a standing ovation.

Kristy caught the Mayor's eye as she patted Cassius's neck over and over.

'Well done,' he mouthed.

She nodded her head. 'Thanks.'

~

BACK IN THE collecting ring a small knot of people had gathered to congratulate them. Kristy's dad produced a carrot from his pocket and gave it to Cassius. Kristy's mum gave the Percheron a hesitant pat.

'It's alright, Mum, he won't hurt you. He's the kindest horse in the world. He's -' Kristy broke off. Her throat throbbed with unshed tears. She brushed a hand across her face. All around people were congratulating them, but Kristy's heart was about to be broken. There was no way Emma wouldn't sell Cassius after their performance today. He'd probably be gone by the end of the week. The thought that she might never see him again was unthinkable. Emotion threatened to overwhelm her. She needed to be on her own.

Her eyes blurry with tears, she jumped off Cassius and threw his reins at her dad. As she ran towards the town hall she heard her mum say, 'What did I do?'

She huddled on the cold concrete steps of the town hall and let the tears fall. She loved Cassius with all her heart. He trusted her. She protected him. Would his new owner look after him like she did? Would they always approach him on his good side so he could see them coming? Talk to him when they went somewhere new so he didn't get frightened? Would they know that he liked being rubbed on the silky soft bit just under his ears? That he adored carrots but wasn't so bothered by apples? That he was a bit stiff on his left rein and needed longer to warm up? That if you blew softly into his nostrils he would blow warm, hay-scented breath back, tickling your neck until you giggled?

In the distance, she heard the Mayor's voice on the tannoy system, but the sound was distorted and impossible to make out over the noise of families chattering and laughing. Applause crackled like static but Kristy ignored it, hugging her knees, her body bunched as tightly as a knot.

'There she is!' cried a familiar voice. Sofia.

Kristy turned to face the wall, flinching as hands grabbed her shoulders.

'Kristy, why did you run away?' The concern in Norah's voice was tinged with exasperation.

She rubbed her eyes and slowly turned towards her three friends. They stood in a semicircle around her.

'Come *on*, Kristy! We've got to ride our lap of honour,' said William.

'What do you mean?' she mumbled.

Sofia held out a hand and pulled Kristy to her feet. She was grinning like a loon. 'We've only gone and won!'

HER DAD WAS STILL HOLDING Cassius and gave her a leg up. She followed the others into the ring and one again they lined up in front of the Mayor. Behind them, the nine other teams filed into the arena. Clasping a large silver cup, a small white envelope and four red rosettes, the Mayor strode over.

'Well done, snowmen! Who shall I give the cup to? Who's the team leader?'

'Norah!' Kristy, Sofia and William chorused. Norah turned crimson but took the cup and envelope graciously.

The Mayor fixed the rosettes to the brow bands of the three ponies. When he reached Cassius, Kristy couldn't stop herself from asking, 'Why us?'

The Mayor scratched Cassius's poll. 'Because you reminded me of my team all those years ago. I saw what good friends you all are, how hard you must have worked. I was impressed that you had the courage to carry on, despite your setback at the start. But most of all I saw how much you were enjoying yourselves. That's what this was all about,' he explained, waving his hands at the arena. 'I wasn't looking for professional dressage riders. I just wanted people to have fun.'

Their lap of honour was a bittersweet moment, and one Kristy knew she would remember forever. Cassius's ears were pricked and his neck was arched as he cantered sedately behind Copper. He was having the time of his life. And Kristy sat tall and proud in the saddle, enjoying his rocking horse canter for what she knew might be the last time.

All too soon they were cantering out of the arena to cheers and applause. The competition had been a huge hit with the crowds and Kristy had a feeling it was likely to become an annual event. She was glad, even though she knew she wouldn't be taking part again.

They decided to ride home in their costumes, waving at everyone they passed. Children stopped and stared, open-mouthed, as the four snowmen on horseback ambled by. By the time they turned down the drive to the stables Kristy's jaw was aching from smiling so much. But it was nothing compared to the ache in her heart.

Back in the yard she busied herself untacking Cassius and making sure he had plenty of hay and water. Once she was satisfied he was settled, she joined the others in the tack room for a well-earned hot chocolate.

Their silver cup had pride of place on the makeshift coffee table. Kristy curled up in an armchair, her fingers clasped around her mug, and listened while the others relived their day.

'You're quiet,' said Norah suddenly.

Kristy felt three pairs of eyes probing her. She was about to bat off Norah's question but then remembered, these were her friends. It was OK to tell them how she was feeling.

'It's Cassius. Emma's going to sell him easily after today, isn't she?'

Kristy stared into her hot chocolate. She didn't notice the other three exchange glances.

'That reminds me,' said Norah briskly, reaching for the envelope tucked in the cup. 'We need to share out our winnings.'

She handed them each £250 in crisp, new notes. Kristy had never seen so much money in her life. But it was worthless to her if it couldn't buy Cassius.

'You could start saving for your own pony,' said Sofia.

Kristy shook her head. 'I don't want another pony. I just want Cassius.'

'Do you even know if anyone's phoned about him?' said William.

'I was too scared to ask Emma earlier,' Kristy admitted.

'Come on, let's go and find her. At least you'll know one way or the other,' said Norah.

'I suppose,' she said doubtfully, following the others into the yard.

Emma was unpacking the Land Rover. Sofia gave Kristy a gentle shove towards her and said, 'Go on, ask her.'

Kristy took a deep breath. 'Emma, have you had much interest in the advert for Cassius?'

Emma slung a haynet over her shoulder. 'Ah, I was going to talk to you about that.'

Kristy went weak at the knees as she braced herself for the worst news. 'You've sold him, haven't you?'

'Yes, I'm afraid I have. But he's going to a four-star home, I promise.'

Kristy thought she heard one of the girls giggle but when she shot a look over her shoulder they were poker-faced. 'Who's bought him?' she said flatly.

Emma rolled her eyes at Sofia. 'Please put the poor girl her out of her misery.'

'You have,' said Sofia.

'What do you mean?'

'You're Cassius's new owner.'

'What?' said Kristy.

'We're giving you our winnings so you can buy him.'

'You're *what*?'

'We took a vote yesterday, actually. Of course, we wouldn't have been able to if we hadn't won. Fortunately, we did. The thirteenth horse was our lucky charm,' grinned William.

A maelstrom of emotions was whirling in Kristy's head. 'It's so kind of you. But I can't take your money.'

Norah stepped forward. 'We wouldn't have stood a chance of winning without you,' she said. 'I would never have been able to vault if you hadn't taught me how.'

'Copper could have been off work for months if you hadn't found him when you did,' added William.

'And I wouldn't have had a costume if you hadn't spent hours helping me make a new one. I'd have had to try to squeeze into the pirate costume I had at primary school, and that would have looked ridiculous,' said Sofia.

'We're doing this because we want to, Kristy,' Norah told her.

Hope flickered like a flame in Kristy's heart and then died. 'But there's no way I can afford his livery fees!'

'What if I said you could work here in return for his keep?' said Emma.

'Seriously?' said Kristy.

'Seriously,' said Emma. 'You're the hardest working stablehand I've ever had. I reckon it's a fair exchange.'

Kristy looked at her boss and her three best friends. 'Are you absolutely sure?'

'Absolutely, totally, one hundred per cent sure,' said Sofia, hugging her tightly.

'How are we going to retain our title of quadrille champions without our lucky charm in the team?' said William, punching her lightly on the shoulder.

'Thank you,' said Kristy, her eyes shining. 'Thank you all so much!'

She sprinted over to Cassius's stable and buried her face in the Percheron's warm neck. She felt luckier than a lottery winner. She had the best friends anyone could ask for and Cassius, the kindest, bravest horse in the world, was absolutely, totally, one hundred per cent hers.

Kristy rubbed the silky soft bit just under her horse's ears. *Her horse*, she marvelled. Would it ever sink in?

Across the yard she could hear the twins arguing about who was going to lead the team the following year. Sofia, as usual, was trying to keep the peace, telling them they could be joint leaders.

Kristy giggled, happier than she thought it was possible to be. 'Joint leaders? Those two?' she spluttered. 'Oh Cassius, can you imagine!'

AFTERWORD

Thank you for reading *The Thirteenth Horse*. If you enjoyed this book it would be great if you could spare a couple of minutes to write a quick review on Amazon. I'd love to hear your feedback!

ABOUT THE AUTHOR

Amanda Wills is the author of The Riverdale Pony Stories, which follow the adventures of pony-mad Poppy McKeever and her beloved Connemara Cloud.

She is also the author of Flick Henderson and the Deadly Game, a fast-paced mystery about a super-cool new heroine who has her sights set on becoming an investigative journalist.

Amanda, a UK-based former journalist who now works part-time as a police press officer, lives in Kent with her husband and fellow indie author Adrian Wills and their sons Oliver and Thomas.

Find out more at www.amandawills.co.uk or at www.-facebook.com/riverdaleseries or follow amandawillsauthor on Instagram.

www.amandawills.co.uk
amanda@amandawills.co.uk

Printed in Great Britain
by Amazon

40082013R00099